THE ADVENTURES

of

BUBBA JONES

TIME-TRAVELING THROUGH ACADIA NATIONAL PARK

The *Adventures of Bubba Jones* is a Registered Trademark ® of Jeff Alt
Library of Congress Cataloging-in-Publication Data On File

ISBN: 9780825308826

For inquiries about volume orders, please contact:
Beaufort Books
27 West 20th Street, Suite 1102
New York, NY 10011
sales@beaufortbooks.com

Published in the United States by Beaufort Books
www.beaufortbooks.com
Distributed by Midpoint Trade Books
www.midpointtrade.com
Printed in the United States of America

Interior design by Jamie Kerry of Belle Étoile Studios
Cover design and illustrations by Hannah Tuohy

A NATIONAL PARK SERIES

THE ADVENTURES

of

BUBBA JONES

TIME-TRAVELING THROUGH ACADIA NATIONAL PARK

BY JEFF ALT

WITH ILLUSTRATIONS BY HANNAH TUOHY

BEAUFORT
BOOKS

BEAUFORT BOOKS
NEW YORK

DISCLAIMER

The Adventures of Bubba Jones is a piece of fiction. All the characters in this book are purely fictional, but the historical and scientific facts about Acadia National Park are true and accurate. The maps are not true to scale. To create this book, the author explored Acadia National Park numerous times on land and sea. He interviewed park experts, combed through local museums and visitor centers, and cross checked the wealth of park facts, to verify accuracy, with sources listed in the bibliography.

Dedicated to Madison & William, two great adventurers.

ACKNOWLEDGEMENTS

I would like to thank the entire Beaufort Books pulishing team, especially Eric Kampmann and Megan Trank, for assembling The Adventures of Bubba Jones into this book and getting it into the hands of those seeking an entertaining and informative adventure. I would also like to thank the following people who were instrumental in the publication of this book: Hannah Tuohy, my illustrator, for her talents in bringing my characters to life; Liz Osborn for her editorial guidance; Carey Kish for sharing some of his favorite Acadia adventures, factual and historical park advice, and for providing some key editing suggestions. I would like to thank the staff from Acadia National Park for providing information and advice, especially Lynne Dominy, Chief of Interpretation. I would like to thank James E. Francis Sr., Director of Cultural & Historic Preservation of the Penobscot Nation, for guidance in providing an accurate depiction of the Wabanaki Native Americans. I would like to thank the Friends of Acadia for providing factual clarification regarding the carriage roads in Acadia National Park. I would like to thank Deborah M. Dyer from the Bar Harbor Historical Society for her historical guidance. I would like to thank

Don Robinson for showing me around Mount Desert Island as I began this project. I would also like to thank Arthur Kampmann for his Acadia National Park guidance as I began this project. I would like to thank my daughter, Madison Alt, for assembling the discussion questions for this edition. And lastly, I would like to thank my wife and children and all of my family and friends that have explored Acadia National Park with me, which helped me develop this book.

Contents

CHAPTER 1

SUNRISE WAKE-UP CALL

"Hey, Bubba Jones, Hug-a-Bug, it's time," Papa Lewis whispered so he wouldn't wake Mom, Dad, Grandma, and the other campers scattered throughout the wooded Blackwoods Campground in the heart of Acadia National Park, Maine. Acadia, a national park spanning 47,000 acres, is one of the top ten most-visited national parks in the country. It boasted over 3 million visitors in 2017 alone. Acadia was first established as Sieur de Monts National Monument in 1916. Then it became Lafayette National Park in 1919 and was finally named Acadia in 1929. It is the oldest national park east of the Mississippi. Located on Mount Desert Island on Maine's eastern seashore, it includes Cadillac Mountain, the tallest mountain along America's east coast. All of this is reason enough to visit this national park! We had originally planned to explore the park next year. Our family loves to explore and experience adventure in the national parks, but Acadia hadn't been on our schedule for this summer. However, we received an urgent message from our cousins who live here on Mount Desert island. They needed our help and fast! We got here as quick as we could, arriving just last night, ready to help. That's what families are for, Mom and Dad reminded us. Now we needed to find out what the problem was and how we could help.

"We're up," I whispered, as Hug-a-Bug and I quietly unzipped our sleeping bags, careful not to wake Mom, Dad, and Grandma, who were sound asleep on the other side of our jumbo-sized family tent.

I stepped outside, and slipped into my boots. I looked down at my watch: 3:30 a.m. It was still dark out, but I could see Papa Lewis' silhouette in the glimmer of moonlight splicing through the trees as he retrieved our egg and ham sandwiches from the cooler. Papa Lewis is our grandfather, named after the famous Meriwether Lewis from the Lewis and Clark Expedition.

"We're not the only ones crazy enough to get up this early," Hug-a-Bug whispered, as she pointed across the road to other campers also quietly preparing to leave their campsites.

We call my sister Jenny "Hug-a-Bug" for her love of everything outdoors. My real name is Tommy, but everyone calls me "Bubba Jones" for my sense for adventure.

Papa Lewis held his index finger to his lips to remind us to be quiet. We topped off our water bottles at the water fountain near the campground bathroom, grabbed our flashlights, hopped in the Jeep, and rolled along a narrow drive out of the campground. In the Jeep, we could talk without whispering.

"Papa Lewis, have you ever met Arthur and Sarah's family?" I asked.

Arthur and Sarah are the cousins that summoned us to Acadia. They are the same ages as Hug-a-Bug and me, but we have never met them. We were on our way to meet them for the first time now.

"Yes, I explored the park with their parents years ago," Papa Lewis replied.

"Why do you think they need our help?" Hug-a-Bug asked.

We had received a coded message from Arthur and Sarah:

KBBA   VLRO   EBIM   FK   XZXAFX

JBBQ   RP   GRIV   BFDEQBBKQE   XQ   PRKOFPB

XQ   LRO   CXSLOFQB   SFBTFKD   MLFKQ

It may seem unusual for most people, especially teenagers, to communicate with family through coded messages, but it's not unusual for our family at all. Our family possesses a very unique ability. If you haven't been along on our other adventures, I'd better explain. You see, we have the ability to time travel into the past. We use our special ability to learn about and to protect our national park wildlands. It's a family secret. I don't think anyone would believe we can time travel anyway though, even if we told them. I still can't believe it myself. But we need to protect our secret from others that might want to use our powers for bad purposes rather than to do good. Hug-a-Bug and I recently inherited the ability to time travel from our Papa Lewis, and we've used this skill to explore two other national parks and to help solve a mystery. Our time-traveling family is scattered across the United States, united in our mission of protecting our wildlands.

The decoded message we received from our relatives in Maine read:

Plain:	NEED	YOUR	HELP	IN	ACADIA
Cipher:	KBBA	VLRO	EBIM	FK	XZXAFX

Plain:	MEET	US	JULY	EIGHTEENTH	AT	SUNRISE
Cipher:	JBBQ	RP	GRIV	BFDEQBBKQE	XQ	PRKOFPB

Plain:	AT	OUR	FAVORITE	VIEWING	POINT
Cipher:	XQ	LRO	CXSLOFQB	SFBTFKD	MLFKQ

Plain	A	B	C	D	E	F	G	H	I	J	K	L	M
Cipher	X	Y	Z	A	B	C	D	E	F	G	H	I	J

Plain	N	O	P	Q	R	S	T	U	V	W	X	Y	Z
Cipher	K	L	M	N	O	P	Q	R	S	T	U	V	W

"I'm not sure what the emergency is, but I'm sure their dad and mom taught them well. They would only send a coded message if there was something wrong," Papa Lewis explained.

"Where are we going to meet them?" I asked Papa Lewis.

"Well, when I was with Fran and Captain George, we watched the sunrise from the top of Cadillac Mountain, the highest mountain on the east coastline. For several months out of the year, Cadillac Mountain is the first place the sun hits in the U.S. each morning," Papa Lewis explained.

"What's the big deal with a sunrise?" Hug-a-Bug asked.

"You'll see," Papa Lewis answered.

We turned onto Cadillac Mountain Road, and our Jeep climbed up a two-lane road to the top. We weren't the first ones up here. As a matter of fact, it seemed like everyone from our campground arrived before us. The parking lot at the top was almost full, but we were early enough to find a parking space.

"I guess their favorite viewing point is no secret," Hug-a-Bug commented as we walked past hundreds of people perched on rocks and sitting on blankets waiting for first light.

"How are we ever going to find them up here?" I asked Papa Lewis.

"Well, there certainly are a lot more people up here now than when I was last here twenty years ago," Papa Lewis said.

"Wow, you can see the ocean!" Hug-a-Bug exclaimed, pointing.

As I took in the view, I could see the glimmer of water in nearly every direction.

"You're looking at Frenchman Bay, and that's Bar Island, Sheep Porcupine Island, and that one over there is Bald Porcupine Island," Papa Lewis explained as he pointed toward several small islands in the distance.

A reddish-yellow glow appeared and lit up the edge of the horizon beyond the little islands. It felt like we were looking out at the edge of the world. Then, the sun appeared, first as a tiny yellow dot on the edge of the ocean, then slowly growing bigger and brighter, until finally it was full daylight.

"Wow!" I said as we stood watching.

As we watched the sun's rays bathe the mountaintop, a feeling of rejuvenation washed over me. During those few moments, we all seemed to forget why we were here. We stood silent, taking in the start of a fresh new day. Soon, the full sun began to rise over the horizon into the sky. The crowd of onlookers began to scatter, some to their cars, others to explore the mountaintop and enjoy the views.

Hug-a-Bug and I scanned the crowd. There was no sign of our cousins Arthur and Sarah that matched the photo we had of them, and no one seemed to be looking around for us either. If our cousins were with their parents, Fran and Captain George, Papa Lewis would've noticed them right away.

"Papa Lewis, our cousins are not up here. What should we do?" I asked.

"Good question, Bubba Jones. This is where Fran, Captain George, your grandma, and I enjoyed the sunrise twenty years ago, but that's not to say that Arthur and Sarah don't have another favorite location" Papa Lewis replied.

"Is there another good spot to view the sunrise besides Cadillac Mountain?" I asked.

"Of course. None as high as Cadillac Mountain, but there are plenty of great spots to watch the sunrise," Papa Lewis replied.

We continued to search for our cousins at the summit of Cadillac Mountain. We followed a line of tourists along a sidewalk and a into gift shop perched on top of Cadillac Mountain. As soon as we stepped through the doorway, a bright yellow envelope taped to the wall behind the cashier caught my eye. On it was written, "Hold for Bubba Jones."

"Look, up on the wall," I whispered to Papa Lewis and Hug-a-Bug as I pointed to the envelope.

I waited in line for the cashier to finish his transaction with the tourist in front of me, and then I stepped up to the counter and said, "That envelope taped to the wall is for me. I'm Bubba Jones."

The cashier looked at me, and then he made eye contact with Papa Lewis standing behind me, and flashed a smile. The man looked like a younger version of our Papa Lewis. He had a beard, and wore a wide brim hat. I looked back at Papa Lewis, and saw he had a grin on his face, too. The cashier pulled the envelope from the wall behind him and handed it me.

"Here you go, Bubba Jones. Keep this safe," the man said, and then he turned his attention to the next person in line and began ringing up their purchases.

"Come on, Bubba Jones and Hug-a-Bug, let's go," Papa Lewis said, striding toward the door.

We followed him outside.

"What was that all about? Who is that man at the register?" I asked Papa Lewis.

"That's Captain George, Arthur and Sarah's dad," Papa Lewis responded.

"Why didn't you say hi or talk with him?" Hug-a-Bug asked.

"Well, he obviously recognized me, but he didn't greet me. I think he wanted us to pretend we didn't know each other. It must have something to do with why they need our help," Papa Lewis explained.

CHAPTER 2

To Cadillac and Beyond

We walked away from the crowd of tourists and sat down on a rock to see what was in the envelope. I tore open the seal and pulled out a folded piece of paper with another coded message:

JBBQ RP LK QEB PELOB MXQE FK YXO
EXOYLO

QLJLOOLT XQ PRKOFPB XQ DIXZFXI BOOXQFZ

XZQ IFHB TB ALKQ HKLT BXZE LQEBO

Hug-a-Bug and I converted the cipher to plain text. It read:

Plain: MEET US ON THE SHORE PATH IN BAR HARBOR

Cipher: JBBQ RP LK QEB PELOB MXQE FK YXO EXOYLO

Plain: TOMORROW AT SUNRISE AT GLACIAL ERRATIC

Cipher QLJLOOLT XQ PRKOFPB XQ DIXZFXI BOOXQFZ

Plain: ACT LIKE WE DON'T KNOW EACH OTHER

Cipher: XZQ IFHB TB ALKQ HKLT BXZE LQEBO

Plain	A	B	C	D	E	F	G	H	I	J	K	L	M
Cipher	X	Y	Z	A	B	C	D	E	F	G	H	I	J

Plain	N	O	P	Q	R	S	T	U	V	W	X	Y	Z
Cipher	K	L	M	N	O	P	Q	R	S	T	U	V	W

"You're right, Papa Lewis, Arthur and Sarah have a different spot to view the Sunrise," Hug-a-Bug said.

"What's a glacial erratic?" I asked Papa Lewis.

"Well, since we're up here and have some time to enjoy the day, I'll show you. There are some glacial erratics right here on Cadillac Mountain. Tuck away the secret message so it doesn't get lost and follow me," Papa Lewis answered as he stood up and led us out onto the Cadillac summit once again.

"You see that large boulder sitting all by itself? How do you think it got there?" Papa Lewis asked pointing to a large rounded boulder that looked like it could go rolling down the mountain at any moment.

"It looks like it just fell out of the sky and landed there," Hug-a-Bug commented.

"Well, not quite. This mountain was formed over 500 million years ago, at the bottom of the ocean. It pushed up through the earth, higher and higher, from a tectonic plate. About 100 million years ago, massive glaciers moved down from present-day Canada and spread as far as the eye can see out into the ocean. As the glaciers moved across the area, they dragged rocks from other mountains with them. When the glaciers retreated, they left these rocks behind, referred to as glacial erratics because they seem so out of place. Notice how this mountain is rounded off? It was once jagged. The glaciers sheared off the tops of these mountains," Papa Lewis said, pointing to the edge of the summit.

"What do you say we go back for a visit?" I suggested.

"Sure. Notice the deep gouged crevices in the granite up here? Those are from the glaciers as they scraped across. Bubba Jones and Hug-a-Bug, take us back nineteen thousand years. The glaciers are receding yet still cover the mountain tops," Papa Lewis directed.

In order to time travel, we need to have our grandfather's leather-bound magic journal with us. Anyone within ten feet of us will go back in time with us, so it's important to make sure we move away from other people. It's also important to time travel out of view of everyone so that we don't freak anybody out, or give away our secret. Imagine seeing someone disappear right before your eyes! The three of us walked away from the crowds at the summit and found some tree cover and bushes to hide behind.

We huddled together and I said, "Take us back nineteen thousand years."

A gust of wind blew, and everything went dark. A cold blast of air smacked my face. We were now wearing thick thermal coats with fur-lined hoods, and goggles. When we time travel, our clothing adjusts to the climate and surroundings of our destination. We were standing on a massive ice glacier. Even with this thermal clothing, I was cold to the bone. Hug-a-Bug's lips were purple, and she stood with her arms wrapped around herself, shivering. I went to take a step toward her to wrap her in a hug to help keep her warm, but my boots were frozen to the ground. I couldn't move.

"This can't be good," I thought as I tried with all my might to break my boots free from the ice.

"This is too cold to survive much longer. Take us back to the present," Papa Lewis yelled above the sound of the wind.

"Take us back to the present," I shouted, clutching the magic time-travel journal.

I felt a jolt as we all free fell. Everything went dark, then lit back up. We were back in the bushes where we had started. The thermal coats, boots, and goggles were gone.

"I'd prefer a warm beach over a glacier any day. That was too cold for me," Hug-a-Bug said.

"Don't you worry, Hug-a-Bug, there is a beach that we will explore while we're here, too," Papa Lewis said.

"There used to be a hotel on Cadillac Mountain called the Green Mountain House. At that time, Cadillac Mountain was called Green Mountain. This was long before Acadia became a park. Not only that, but you could take a train or a horse and wagon to the top," Papa Lewis explained.

"Did you say train?" I asked

"Yep! The hotel was built in 1866 and then in 1883, the Green Mountain Cog Railway began service from Eagle Lake, about a mile from here, to the top of Green Mountain," Papa Lewis explained.

"What's a cog railway?" I asked.

"A cog railway engine pushes rail cars up the mountain, and it has an extra wheel in the center with metal teeth that mesh into the track to keep the train from rolling backward. It's very similar to a modern-day roller coaster clicking along as it chugs up the first big hill," Papa Lewis explained.

Hug-a-Bug smiled with anticipation, knowing we were going to time travel back for a ride on the Cog Railway. I could tell she thought it would be like a roller coaster ride.

We huddled back behind some bushes, out of view of tourists once again, and Hug-a-Bug said, "Take us back to the Green Mountain Cog Railway in July of 1883."

A gust of wind blew, and everything went dark as we were thrust down the mountain. When I regained my vision, we were seated on wooden benches in a covered rail car with open sides. Women wearing ankle-length dresses and men in suits, ties, and wide brim hats stood in line with suitcases, waiting to board the train. I hopped off the train to take a look around. We were stopped next to a large lake. A puff of steam billowed out of the train engine's smokestack. A man inside the coal car tossed logs into the engine.

The conductor collected tickets and then shouted, "All aboard!" It was just like in the movies!

I hopped back up to my seat as the engine wheels began to slowly turn and push us up the mountain. The metallic click of the cogwheel ticked away. The ride was slow-going, but very scenic. Just like Papa Lewis explained, it felt like we were chugging up a roller coaster hill as each tooth of the cogwheel locked onto the track.

"Wow! This is the ultimate way to summit Cadillac Mountain," Hug-a-Bug shouted with excitement.

"Young lady, this is Green Mountain, not Cadillac Mountain," a woman seated behind us corrected her.

"Yes ma'am, you're right. I don't know why I said Cadillac," Hug-a-Bug responded.

"That's quite all right, young lady. I just want to make sure you have your facts straight," the woman replied.

For the rest of the ride up to the summit, the woman, who held a college degree, a rarity for woman in the late 1800s, gave us quite an education about the history of the area.

"Young lady, let me tell you about this beautiful area. The French were the first Europeans to discover Mount Desert Island when Samuel de Champlain sailed here in 1604. He named it *Isle des Monts Deserts*. Natives already inhabited the island when they arrived. In 1613, French Jesuits made friends with the local natives and established a mission. But they were driven out by the English. You see, the French and English competed for this land and for much of the land in North America back then. For a long time after that, though, neither the French nor English bothered much with Mount Desert Island until 1688, when a French explorer by the name of Antoine de La Mothe, Sieur de Cadillac, was granted ownership of thousands of acres of land, including Mount Desert Island. However, he and his wife didn't stay long. They left for the Great Lakes, and he founded Detroit. Maybe that is where you got the name 'Cadillac,'" the woman offered.

"Yes ma'am, I believe you're right. I must have just got my history a little jumbled," Hug-a-Bug agreed.

I sat on the train with a huge grin for the entire ride up the mountain. Papa Lewis had taught Hug-a-Bug and me all of the history behind this area on the ride up to Maine. I knew Hug-a-Bug wanted to show off her knowledge, but she held back for fear of saying something else about an event that had not yet occurred in 1883, like the Cadillac car, made by General Motors, whose name was inspired by Sieur de Antoine de la Mothe Cadillac. I laughed to myself just thinking how this very educated woman would have reacted if Hug-a-Bug had mentioned the Cadillac car. The woman would have thought poor Hug-a-Bug was completely out of her mind. There are some pitfalls that go with time travel!

In less than an hour, we arrived at the summit. The Cadillac Mountain summit, which in present day is devoid of manmade structures other than a small tourist center, was now graced with a grand hotel with a wrap-around porch, the Green Mountain House. It had a rooftop lookout that Papa Lewis called a widow's watch. Groups of men, women, and children sat outside on the covered porch. We stepped inside and encountered more well-dressed people sitting on fancy couches and chairs, talking and sipping drinks. We located the stairs to the widow's watch and climbed up to have a look. When we reached it, we stepped out to the rail and were rewarded with the same beautiful view of the sea and the islands that we had been graced with at sunrise. While we took in the view, a teenage boy emerged from the stairs and joined us at the rail, gazing out to sea.

"Papa Lewis, why do they call this a widow's watch?" Hug-a-Bug asked.

"A widow's watch, or widow's walk, as it is sometimes called, was designed to allow wives of sailors to watch for their spouses while they were at sea. Many sailors have been lost at sea, which is why they refer to it as a widow's watch. But it also makes a great vantage point when you're not worried about losing your loved one at sea," Papa Lewis explained.

After a few minutes of enjoying the view, we walked back downstairs and kept to ourselves to make sure we didn't have any more slips of the tongue after Hug-a-Bug's gaffe about the name of the mountain on the Cog Railway. We slipped over to some bushes out of view.

Hug-a-Bug took the journal from my pocket and said, "Take us back to the present."

A gust of wind blew, everything went dark, and when I regained focus, we were sitting in the bushes wearing our modern clothes once again.

"That was fun," I said, and Hug-a-Bug smiled and nodded in agreement.

"Cadillac, Cadillac, Cadillac. I just had to say that!" Hug-a-Bug stated exasperatedly.

"You covered for it well after your slip-up, Hug-a-Bug. We certainly don't want to cause any disturbance of the past, but you handled your Cadillac mistake well," Papa Lewis reassured her.

"Thank you," Hug-a-Bug responded.

"The Cog Railway only lasted a few years and then went out of service. In 1918, Green Mountain was renamed Cadillac Mountain after Anotoine de la Moth Sieur de Cadillac, the French explorer that the woman told you about," Papa Lewis explained. We took a stroll along the Cadillac Summit Loop Trail and then we took a long hike along the North Ridge Trail, down the mountain and back up again. The hike back up to the Summit of Cadillac Mountain took some time.

After a scenic and exhausting hike, we returned to our Jeep and drove down the mountain, loaded with stories to share with Mom, Dad, and Grandma.

CHAPTER 3

POPOVER MYSTERY

I rode in the front seat to help Papa Lewis navigate.

"Papa Lewis, that woman kept talking about Mount Desert Island. Where is that?" Hug-a-Bug asked.

"Acadia National Park is on a small island called Mount Desert Island. Locals simply refer to it as MDI. Nearly half of MDI is now Acadia National Park, with the remainder of the island in private ownership. You can get around about sixty percent of the park on the Park Loop Road, but in the summer, it gets busy with traffic. We're going to meet up with your parents and grandma at the Jordan Pond House," Papa Lewis explained.

We descended Cadillac Mountain Road in low gear, and I directed Papa Lewis to turn left towards the Jordan Pond House.

"Your grandma loves this place, and I bet you will, too," Papa Lewis commented, pulling into the parking lot for the Jordan Pond House. We saw Dad, Mom, and Grandma step off a tour bus emblazoned with the words "Island Explorer." A line of tourists stood nearby under a tree-shaded pergola until everyone had filed off the bus. Then the tourists under the pergola boarded the Island Explorer and it drove off.

"The Island Explorer is a great way to get around the park without having to drive or worry about parking," Dad said.

"That's good to know, Clark. I think we should use the Island Explorer then. There are a lot more people in the park now than the last time I was here with your grandma 20 years ago. The bus should help us get around faster," Papa Lewis responded.

My dad is named Clark after the famous William Clark of the Lewis and Clark Corps of Discovery. When Papa Lewis and my dad are on adventure together, they are known as Lewis and Clark.

When my mom is on adventure, we call her Petunia for her love of flowers. Grandma is just Grandma or Grandma Jones.

"We have a reservation," Grandma said with excitement as we approached the hostess to give our name.

"Lewis and Clark, your table is ready. Please, follow

me." The hostess turned and led us outside behind the building, where rows of wooden tables and benches were set up across the lawn, overlooking a pond. In the distance, we could see the mountains.

"That's Jordan Pond and the mountains you see are called The Bubbles," Grandma said, gesturing toward the amazing view.

We updated Dad, Mom, and Grandma of our Cadillac Mountain adventure and let them know about the envelope with the new message to meet our cousins on the Shore Path in Bar Harbor at sunrise tomorrow.

"Something is up. We ran into Captain George at the gift shop on Cadillac Mountain. He was working the register, and smiled at me when he saw me, but didn't offer a greeting, and treated me as if I was just another customer. He was the one who gave Bubba Jones the envelope with the new message that says we need to act like we don't know each other when we're in public," Papa Lewis told Grandma.

"That is strange. Something must be wrong. I hope everyone is okay," Grandma answered.

"I think all of us should meet up with them tomorrow morning," Papa Lewis replied.

"That fits right in with our lodging plans for tonight. I booked a hotel for us in Bar Harbor," Clark said.

"Perfect," Papa Lewis replied.

A server approached our table, handed us menus, and filled our glasses with water.

"I'll be back in a moment to take your order," he said

as he walked over to another table to check on them.

"This is the only restaurant in Acadia. They're famous for tea and popovers," Grandma said.

"What's a popover?" Hug-a-Bug asked.

"A popover is a hollow roll made from egg batter. They're baked in muffin pans. The rolls pop up and over when they bake, which is why they call them popovers. They're really good with strawberry jam and creamery butter. Thomas and Nellie McIntire began serving them here in 1895 to the wealthy tourists. Back then, some of the richest people in America built mansions here on MDI. They were known as rusticators," Grandma explained.

"Let's go back and try Thomas and Nellie's popovers to see if they taste like the ones we're about to eat," I suggested.

"Yum! Sounds great," Hug-a-Bug said, and all of us stood up and walked behind some trees near Jordan Pond.

I held the journal in my hand and said, "Take us back to Jordan Pond House in July of 1895."

A gust of wind blew us, everything went dark, and then suddenly, we were there. I looked down to see what I was wearing, then looked at the others. I was dressed in a suit and tie just like Papa Lewis and Dad. Hug-a-Bug, Grandma, and Mom wore ankle-length dresses and sun hats. We walked out from behind the trees. The building was different.

"The original Jordan Pond House burned down in 1979 and was rebuilt," Papa Lewis explained in a whisper.

A man approached us and said, "Welcome, I'm Thomas McIntire. Will you be joining us for tea and popovers?"

"Yes please," Grandma replied.

"Right this way," Thomas said, leading us to a table.

Moments later, servers arrived and assembled plates of popovers in front of each of us, along with strawberry jam and butter. Then they filled our cups with hot tea. I spread jam on my popover and gobbled it down. It was awesome! I looked around the table and saw that everyone else had finished their popovers, too. Papa Lewis pulled some change from his pocket and dropped it on the table to cover our tab, then we all stood up to walk over to the trees to travel back to the present. That's when I noticed the teenage boy sitting by himself at another table. He was the same boy that climbed up to the widow's watch at the Green Mountain House when we rode the Cog Railway up the mountain. I was just about to point him out to Hug-a-Bug, but she had noticed him, too.

"Bubba Jones, that's the same boy that was at the widow's watch at the Green Mountain House. What's he doing here? That's weird. . .to time travel to two different periods and see the same kid," Hug-a-Bug said.

"I agree, that's strange. Probably nothing to worry about though. Let's go back to the present," I stated.

A gust of wind blew, everything went dark for a moment, and then we found ourselves back in the present day. We filed out from behind the trees and returned to our table. I was excited to eat another pop-over. The server came to take our order, and a short while later, brought us our popovers with butter and strawberry jam, and poured us each a cup of hot tea; it was just like it had been in 1895. Not only did the popovers look the same as they had in 1895, they tasted just as delicious!

"These are awesome, Grandma! Just like Nellie and Thomas' were in 1895," I stated.

The server overheard my comment and responded, "Wow, you certainly know your history, young man."

"You wouldn't believe how much I know this history!" I said with a grin.

CHAPTER 4

SECRET SUNRISE

We drove the Park Loop Road a short distance into the town of Bar Harbor as Papa Lewis told us more about the area.

"Mount Desert Island is not that big. It is made up of a few small towns, along with Acadia National Park. Many of the tourists that visit Acadia stay in Bar Harbor," Papa Lewis explained.

Papa Lewis turned our Jeep onto a two-lane road and within a few minutes, we passed a sign that read "Bar Harbor." The streets were lined with large trees and old homes, many with bed and breakfast signs on the front lawns. We turned onto Main Street and passed a little park. The street was lined with tourist shops and restaurants. July is the height of tourist season and hundreds of people filled the sidewalks, carrying ice cream cones and shopping bags. I caught a glimpse of the Acadia National Park Information Center across the street from the town park aka Village Green. We rolled along with traffic, and I could see a large ship out in the distance. A loud fog horn belched out, "Whoomph, whoomph."

"Until railroads became common, the primary method of travel to Acadia National Park and Bar Harbor was by ship. That's a cruise line docked out in the harbor. That's where a lot of the tourists filling the sidewalks are from," Papa Lewis explained.

We turned onto a small drive that followed the ocean shore and pulled up to a hotel right on the shoreline. Several small boats bobbed in the harbor, and a large sail boat, the Margaret Todd, a four masted schooner, was docked at a wooden pier in front of the hotel. The view was amazing.

"This is our home for the night. Our room has a terrace overlooking the Shore Path. We can all roll out of bed right before sunrise to meet up with Arthur, Sarah, Captain George, and Fran in our pajamas!

We all hopped out of the Jeep and paused to drink in the ocean view.

After a moment, Papa Lewis broke our reverie, saying "Those smaller vessels anchored offshore are lobster boats. You haven't experienced Mount Desert Island until you've experienced the ocean that surrounds it, and that includes eating some of the lobster brought in by those boats. You haven't been to Acadia if you haven't tried the lobster," Papa Lewis said.

"It's so pretty here. I feel special to be here," Hug-a-Bug said.

"That's probably why it is a favorite vacation destination among the rich and famous, as well as everyday folk like us. Mount Desert Island is for everyone to enjoy," Papa Lewis explained. The more Papa Lewis told us about the area, the more it sunk in that the ocean is just as much a part of Acadia National Park as the island.

After we checked into our rooms, we enjoyed a dinner of sandwiches with sliced cucumber and carrots on the hotel terrace overlooking the ocean. After we finished, Grandma slipped into the room and reemerged holding cheesecake dripping with blueberry syrup and bursting with blueberries.

"Wow! Thanks, Grandma and Mom," I said.

"This was all your grandma," Mom said as she helped Grandma slice the cake, placing each slice on a separate paper plate and passing them around until everybody had one.

"A trip to Acadia just isn't complete without some Maine blueberries, and I just love this cheesecake," Grandma added.

"This is awesome! Thank you, Grandma," Hug-a-Bug said between bites.

Having been up since 3 a.m., I was ready to fall asleep

shortly after dinner. Morning would arrive all too soon with another predawn wake-up call, so we crawled into our beds. We slept with the terrace door open to enjoy the cool ocean breeze. I drifted off to sleep to the sound of ocean waves crashing against the rocky seashore.

"Bubba Jones, Hug-a-Bug, wake up. It's time," Dad said standing over us in the dimly-lit room.

I sat up in bed and was greeted by a gibbous moon in an indigo sky above, its reflection shimmering on the ocean's surface below. As Mom had suggested, we stayed in our pajamas so we could crawl right back into bed for another few hours of sleep after our sunrise rendezvous. We pulled on our shoes and jackets. I tucked my time-travel journal into my jacket pocket, and we slipped out into the hall and crept down the corridor, through the hotel doors, and outside onto the Shore Path. Moments later, as I squinted into the darkness, I could just barely make out the silhouettes of four people standing further down the path, near a massive boulder. The boulder rested on a slight downward slope, making it look as if one hard shove might send it tumbling into the sea below.

I paused on the trail, as the others caught up to me. "I think that's them," I whispered, pointing out the figures ahead, "standing next to that big boulder; that must be the glacial erratic they mentioned."

"Remember, we need to act as if we don't know them. Let them communicate to us first," Papa Lewis whispered back.

We climbed over a small retaining wall and walked

along the rock-strewn beach toward the figures. The glacial erratic loomed over us. There was a faint glow cast over the beach; the first hint of the sunrise. In the dim light, I could see that the two kids standing there were Arthur and Sarah, dressed in pajamas just like us.

"Would you take our picture?" our cousin Arthur asked.

"Sure," I said taking the smartphone out of his extended hand, while reminding myself not to acknowledge that we were here to meet with them.

I stepped back a few feet to get everyone in focus with the camera, and just as I was about to snap the shot, I noticed a small piece of paper taped to the phone screen. It read, "Meet us in the restaurant at your hotel, in the private banquet room, for breakfast at 9 a.m."

I thought to myself that the note sure was a clever way to communicate without anyone knowing. These Maine cousins of ours were pretty high-speed! I peeled the note off the phone and slipped it into my pocket so that Arthur would know I had received it.

I snapped some pictures, then handed the phone back to Arthur and handed him our camera to take a shot of us, just like friendly tourists might do. Papa Lewis, Grandma, Dad, Mom, Hug-a-Bug, and I gathered in front of the glacial erratic and Arthur took our picture, then handed the camera back to me. Moments later, the sky turned pale pink, and a few more tourists stood along the path to watch the sun emerge on the distant horizon, casting its beams across the ocean all the way to our feet. It felt like a fresh new beginning, just like the feeling I had yesterday as we experienced the sunrise from Cadillac Mountain. The big difference was there were fewer tourists here and no traffic. The sun continued to rise above the water up into the sky, marking the beginning of a new day.

"That was amazing!" Hug-a-Bug breathed.

"It sure was!" Grandma agreed as she embraced Hug-a-Bug with a hug.

Without saying a word to give away our connection to Arthur, Sarah, Fran, and Captain George, we climbed back up to the path and walked to our hotel room for a few more hours of sleep. I fell back asleep as soon as my head hit the pillow.

CHAPTER 5

TIME TO SOLVE A MYSTERY

It was 8:30 a.m., time for us to get up again. We quickly got dressed for the day and made our way through the inner halls of the inn to the private meeting room. The room was oval in shape, with a wraparound balcony from which we had a stunning view of Frenchman's Bay. The center of the room featured a table draped with a white tablecloth and eight place settings of fine china.

"Wow, this is fancy," Hug-a-Bug commented.

"Look at this view," I chimed in.

"The Bar Harbor Inn is loaded with history," Papa Lewis said.

Before Papa Lewis had a chance to expand on the

history, Captain George, Fran, Arthur, and Sarah filed into the room, each carrying covered dishes. Without saying a word, they all set the dishes down on the table. Captain George and Arthur shut the doors which closed off the room from the hall.

"We are safe to speak here. We have friends watching the hall who will let us know if anyone unexpected comes near," Captain George explained.

For several minutes, Papa Lewis, Grandma, Mom, Dad, Fran, and Captain George hugged, talked, and got reacquainted with each other. Hug-a-Bug and I had never met Arthur and Sarah, so the four of us stood looking out the window at the amazing view of the Atlantic Ocean. I told Arthur I was impressed with his slyness in slipping the note to me on his phone.

"Let's all sit down and eat before the food gets cold," Fran announced.

She exited the room and returned with a tray holding a thermos of hot coffee, a pitcher of milk, water, and orange juice. She closed the door and locked it behind her.

"What's going on?" Papa Lewis asked, looking at Captain George.

"Someone stole my time-travel pocket watch, and until we get it back, we are all in danger. Whoever took it could go back in time and change history. We need your help," Captain George explained.

I couldn't imagine losing our time-travel ability. Just the thought of it caused me to place my hand onto my time-travel journal to make sure it was snug in my pocket.

"Wow! How did the watch get stolen?" I asked.

"Eight days ago, we were on a time-travel adventure to George Dorr's farm. All that remains is the foundation of his home," Arthur began to explain.

"Who is George Dorr?" I interrupted.

"George Dorr is known as the 'Father of Acadia.' He led the effort to create Acadia National Park. The ruins of his home are set back in a wooded area along the coastline that overlooks Compass Harbor and the Porcupine Islands, less than a mile from here. It's part of Acadia National Park. We had just returned from the past to the present on our traditional Sunday afternoon time-travel adventure. We decided to do something out of the ordinary and visit George Dorr's home. After all, it was his energy and hard work that created Acadia National Park. The four of us were gathered near the ruins of the foundation. I set my time-travel pocket watch down on the ledge of the foundation so I could retie my shoes. When I looked back up to retrieve the watch, it was gone and I could hear the snapping sound of twigs from someone running away through the forest. We thought we were alone out there. We always check carefully to make sure no one else is around before we time travel. But someone must have been there, and we didn't see them. We unwittingly took whoever it was on our time-travel trip. They must have seen me use the time-travel watch, and then when they saw it sitting on the foundation ledge, they took it. We don't know what to do. We've been unable to time travel since," Arthur explained.

"That's why we reached out to you. Every minute that our time-travel ability is in the wrong hands, there is a risk that history could be altered, and that could disrupt the present and the future. We need to find this person and get that time-travel watch back, and fast! The family council recommended your family to help us. They told us great things about how Bubba Jones, Hug-a-Bug, and all of you have solved some big mysteries in other national parks. Can you help us?" Captain George asked.

"That's why we're here. We're all in this together to protect and preserve our national parks and wildlands. We will do everything we can to get that watch back," Papa Lewis responded.

"Absolutely! Whatever we can do to help, let us know. I didn't know there was a family council," Bubba Jones said.

"Yes, the council is activated whenever someone in our time-travel family anywhere across the country has a crisis. It was created for this precise situation. You activate the family crisis council by telling an elder in your clan about your situation. If the elder agrees that the situation is a threat to the national parks, our wildlands, or our time travel, the council is activated. Until this issue is resolved, the council will remain activated," Papa Lewis explained.

"Wow, I learn more about our time-travel family every day. Who's on the family council?" I asked.

"It's a secret. The members rotate, and even they don't

know who the others are until they meet for a crisis. But enough about that for now. We need to solve this situation," Papa Lewis stated.

"Count me in," Hug-a-Bug said.

"Me, too," Dad replied.

"That goes for me, too," Mom chimed in.

"Let's get that watch back," Grandma said.

"I knew we could count on your clan, Lewis. Since we don't know who this person is, we can't let our relationship with you be known. That's why we met here. Fran hosts events for this hotel, and she could reserve this room. When I retired from the service, I began to volunteer for the park and fill in as a backup staff member for the park concessionaire that runs the bookstores and gift shops. So, I will be able to help secure some other meeting locations if that becomes necessary. Whoever took that watch could come after your time-travel ability as well. We should continue to meet in secret and communicate through the family secret code until we know more," Captain George explained.

Fran pulled the lids off the silver trays of food and said, "Dig in."

The smell of sausage and pancakes permeated my thoughts. Wow! I didn't know where to start. There was a mound of steamy blueberry pancakes, bacon, scrambled eggs, fresh Maine blueberries, and warm Maine blueberry syrup. The room fell silent as we all dug in. As I ate, I began to think deeper on what to do from here.

"What does your pocket watch look like? Do you have

a picture of it?" I asked Arthur.

"It's a silver pocket watch with a chain. Etched into the outside cover is the inscription 'Learn from the past to protect the future.' We have an old photograph of my great-grandpa holding it. But the photo is not that clear. The watch has been in our clan since the Revolutionary War," Arthur explained.

"Can we go to George Dorr's homestead to look around and time travel back to the same period you did?" I asked.

"That would be a great idea. We should travel separately and meet up at the foundation ruins. We need to make sure we are not followed. To communicate with us, leave an encrypted message in a sealed envelope addressed to Fran at the front desk of the hotel. She has a mailbox there. We will leave notes for you in Fran's mailbox. They will be addressed to Bubba Jones," Captain George explained.

After breakfast, Captain George spread a map on the table and reviewed directions with us. After agreeing on the mission, everyone stood up from the table. Captain George embraced Papa Lewis in a bear hug and said, "It's good to see you again, my friend. Too bad it's not under better circumstances."

"We'll get to the bottom of this," Papa Lewis assured Captain George.

CHAPTER 6

GONE IN A POOF!

We all said our goodbyes to Arthur, Sarah, Fran, and Captain George and headed back to our hotel room. We filled our daypacks with water and snacks, piled into the Jeep, and we were off.

In minutes, we pulled off the road at the outskirts of town onto a narrow drive and parked the Jeep. We got out of the vehicle and followed the Compass Harbor Trail into the forest. In a few minutes, the trail ended at the ruins of George Dorr's home. All that remained were a red brick terrace and some portions of the foundation walls. It was a peaceful place beneath the shade of the trees and with the rhythmic sound of ocean waves off in the distance. We followed the sound out to a beautiful view of the coastline. After taking in the view, we walked back to the ruins to wait for our cousins.

"What a place to live! Why didn't they preserve Mr. Dorr's home?" I asked Papa Lewis.

"The home was built by his wealthy parents and completed in 1880. It was a 30-room summer house. After George died in 1944, the home fell into disrepair and was razed. I'm not sure why they didn't preserve it. My guess is that George Dorr's focus was on preserving Acadia National Park and the house wasn't considered historically important at the time," Papa Lewis answered.

We heard someone or something approaching from the woods, and Arthur, Sarah, Fran, and Captain George came into view. At first, they pretended not to know us. They split up and searched all around the property to look for the time-travel pocket watch and to make sure no one else was in the area. After finding neither interlopers nor pocket watch, Arthur and his family dropped the pretense and greeted us.

"Are you ready to time travel back to the same time period we went to right before I lost the watch?" Arthur asked.

"Let's do this," I answered.

We all gathered in a circle in front of the foundation ruins, and Arthur made another quick scan around us to make sure no one else was in sight.

"The coast is clear Bubba Jones. Take us back to July 15th, 1916," Arthur directed.

"Takes us back to July 15th, 1916," I repeated as I held the time-travel journal.

Everything went dark, a gust of wind blew us backward, then it became light again. We were now standing in the front yard of a majestic mansion. It had a large covered front porch, and it was three stories tall. We were all dressed up, with the boys and men decked out in suit jackets, ties, and newsboy hats, while the women wore long dresses and sun hats.

"Mr. Dorr just celebrated the beginning of his success in creating Acadia National Park. Years earlier, 1901 to be exact, Mr. Dorr joined forces with the Hancock County Trustees of Public Reservations to preserve the area as a park. Over time, they bought 6,000 acres of land and gave it to the federal government to preserve for public use. In 1916, President Woodrow Wilson created the Sieur de Monts National Monument," Captain George explained in a whisper.

Arthur turned and walked towards the ocean, away from the mansion. Everyone followed him out to the ocean view. As we approached the shore, we saw a man standing there quietly enjoying the view. He had a bushy mustache. He wore a wide brim boater, suit jacket, vest, and bow tie.

"That's George Dorr. Let's go meet him," Captain George whispered to us.

We were just about to approach Mr. Dorr, when I

noticed a boy standing further down the shoreline. The boy was looking down at something and didn't see us. It was the same teenage boy we had seen at the widow's watch on Green Mountain, and at the Jordan Pond House. I tugged at Hug-a-Bug's arm and tapped Papa Lewis on the shoulder. Once I had their attention, I pointed to the boy. Without saying a word, I motioned for everyone to back away towards the house. When were out of sight of the boy, I stopped.

"That boy was on Green Mountain when we time traveled to ride the Cog Railway, and he was at the Jordan Pond House when we traveled back to try the original popover, and now he's here, too!" I exclaimed.

"He was in the past the day my time-travel watch was stolen, too," Arthur said.

We all looked at each other, then everyone seemed to come to the same conclusion at once.

"That boy must be a time traveler. Is he related? Do you know him?" I asked looking at Arthur and Sarah.

"No, he's not from our clan, and we don't know him. We're the only time-travel clan in all of Maine. When I saw him on our time travel here, the day my pocket watch was stolen, I thought he looked familiar, but I couldn't place him. He must be the one who stole my watch! Let's go after him!" Arthur declared as he charged off towards the shoreline where we had seen the boy.

We followed Arthur, while trying to stay out of Mr. Dorr's view. As we closed in on the boy, I could see that he was holding a silver pocket watch in his hand. Arthur was almost within reach of the boy, and caught his attention. The boy looked up at Arthur.

"That's my watch. Can I have it back?" Arthur said, holding out his hand.

Time seemed to stand still for a moment, then the boy turned and ran. Arthur, Sarah, Hug-a-Bug, and I followed him. The terrain along the shoreline was steep and rocky, forcing us to slow down so as not to lose our balance and fall into the ocean. Arthur was gaining on the boy when a gust of wind suddenly knocked us back, and the boy disappeared into thin air.

"He traveled back to the present. We need to travel back to the present now!" Arthur cried, an edge of panic in his voice.

We ran back to Captain George, Fran, Papa Lewis, Grandma, Dad, and Mom. Even with all this commotion, Mr. Dorr never noticed.

"We have to go. Get in a circle," I said.

Everyone quickly joined hands safely out of view of Mr. Dorr.

"Take us back to the present," I stated holding onto my journal.

Everything went dark and a strong wind knocked us back. After a moment, it brightened again, and we were standing in front of the ruins of Mr. Dorr's home. We all fanned out to look for the boy. After several minutes, we regrouped. He was nowhere to be found.

"When you time travel separately, it's easy to miss each other. The boy could have time traveled from a different location near here, and he would have returned to that same location. He also had a few minutes head start. Since he knew he was being pursued, he probably kept running," Papa Lewis explained.

We searched the entire area for almost an hour before giving up. The boy was nowhere to be found. We found a place to sit along the shore, with a great view of the Atlantic and out of earshot of any bystanders.

"The good news is that we know who has your pocket watch. We know what he looks like. We know that he has time traveled to some of the more historical sites in the park. He's probably confused as to how we could time travel without that pocket watch. Now, we need to hatch a plan to get that watch back," I said.

"This changes our game plan. Since we know who it is, I don't think we need to worry about our two families being seen together. We should stick together. We still don't know what his motive is for stealing the watch. He could simply be wowed by the prospect of being able to go back in time. But he could be up to something sinister. We also don't know if he's working alone or with others. It appears, so far, that he is simply exploring the park's history and taking advantage of the opportunity to time travel. It seems likely we'll run into him again by simply exploring all the highlights of the park. I think we should try that first to see if we can get the pocket watch back. So, I say that we give our Jones cousins a red carpet Acadia time-travel adventure!" Captain George finished, his face split with a wide grin.

"Let me get this straight. You want us to forget that my watch, the watch that has been handed down through the family for generations, the watch that I can't time travel without, the watch that in the wrong hands allows an interloper to time travel and possibly change the past and mess up the present, has been stolen...and just go have fun?! You want us to just take off on an Acadia time-travel adventure?!" Arthur asked his dad incredulously.

"Relax. There is nothing to be gained by worrying. That just causes unnecessary stress. But there is a lot to be gained by developing a plan and executing it. Our plan just happens to involve living in the moment. Or should I say the past?" Captain George replied, playfully tousling Arthur's hair.

Arthur appeared to be considering his dad's suggestion, and after a moment, he sighed, then gave a sheepish smile and visibly relaxed.

"I guess you're right," he replied.

We all felt a little more at ease with this idea. It made sense.

"If we encounter this boy on any of our adventures, we should befriend him. We should find out his name and get any personal information we can," Captain George explained.

"Why should we make friends with a thief? How can we trust a person like that?" Sarah asked.

"You're right, Sarah. We can't trust him. But we can't report a stolen time-travel pocket watch to the authorities, either. The police will think we're out of our minds!

But you saw what happened when Arthur confronted the boy; he got scared and ran," Captain George explained.

"I agree, let's explore Acadia and get your watch back," Papa Lewis stated.

CHAPTER 7

THE REAL FOUNDERS OF MOUNT DESERT ISLAND

Hug-a-Bug and I were excited to spend time with Sarah and Arthur without having to pretend we didn't know them; we could act like real cousins! We checked out of the hotel and moved into our cousins' house on the outskirts of Bar Harbor. We planned to base camp out of their house for a few days while we followed Captain George's plan. They lived in a two-story house, set back off the road on a heavily wooded lot, just a few minutes away from the park entrance. As soon as we stepped into their home, a black and white dog ran between my legs and wagged its tail, full of energy and excitement. The dog looked me right in the eye with its head cocked as if to say, "Look, I know you're a time traveler, so you better take me on your next adventure; don't leave me out!"

"That's Cadillac. He's a border collie. Acadia National Park is very dog-friendly; they just ask that you keep your dog on a leash in the park. Cadillac goes with us on most of our park adventures except for the trails that require hand-over-hand climbing. He's well-trained and has time traveled with us many times," Arthur said.

"That's awesome! I like his name. I've never time traveled with a dog before," I said as I stooped down to pet Cadillac, stroking his ears and the top of his head.

Hug-a-Bug came over and pet him, too.

"Wow! It must be awesome to live right here with the park and all the opportunity for adventure right outside your door!" Hug-a-Bug said to Arthur and Sarah.

"Yeah, we've had a blast exploring Mount Desert Island. Arthur and I just inherited dad's time-travel pocket watch, and he's been coaching us on how to use it. But we were already seasoned time travelers. We've time traveled all over the island with our parents, ever since we were little kids," Sarah explained.

Arthur unfolded a map of Acadia National Park on the kitchen table, and we began to make plans to explore the park, time-travel style.

"Let's start our park adventure with a visit to the Abbe

Museum at Sieur de Monts Spring and then we'll visit the newer modern Abbe Museum here in Bar Harbor. This will help give everyone an understanding of the culture, history, and archaeology of the Wabanaki people," Arthur suggested as he pointed his finger at Sieur de Monts on the park map.

"Who are the Wabanaki people?" Hug-a-Bug asked.

"Arthur and I have learned about the Wabanaki people in school and we've visited the Abbe museums with our class and with our parents. It's one of my favorite subjects in school. The Wabanaki, also known as 'People of the Dawnland,' are native Americans, that are made up of four tribes. The Wabanaki people have inhabited the land of Acadia National Park and Mount Desert Island for 12,000 years, long before the Europeans arrived. They refer to Mount Desert Island as 'Pemetic' which means 'range of mountains.' Today, the Wabanaki people continue to enjoy Acadia National Park and Mount Desert Island. This area remains sacred to their ancestry and culture," Sarah explained.

"As parents, we like the fact that our school curriculum includes the teachings of Maine native American history and culture. Our kids have learned so much and us grownups have learned quite a bit too," Captain George stated with a pleasing smile.

"That's great. Learning about local history and culture is so important to help us understand our world," Papa Lewis responded.

"Let's go, this sounds like a fascinating adventure," I said.

"That sounds like a great idea. While we're doing that, Fran is going to take Petunia and Grandma Jones to the fresh market to pick up dinner. We will all meet back here. If anything goes wrong, remember to check Fran's mailbox at the hotel for messages," Captain George said.

Arthur, Sarah, Captain George, Papa Lewis, Dad, Hug-a-Bug, and I walked down to the village green, and hopped on the Island Explorer headed to Sieur de Monts Spring. Arthur filled us in on some more facts and history as we rode along.

"Today, the Wabanaki people remain an important part of our community. Each of the four Wabanaki tribes maintain their own reservation spread out across Maine," Arthur explained.

"Ever since Arthur went on a summer field trip to an active archeological site, he has wanted to become an archeologist and he's fascinated with the discoveries of Dr. Abbe," Captain George explained.

"Who's Dr. Abbe?" Hug-a-Bug asked

"You're about to find out," Sarah said with a grin.

The bus pulled into a parking area in front of the Sieur de Monts Spring Nature Center and Wild Gardens. We filed off the bus and followed Arthur and Sarah past the nature center along a paved path.

"We'll visit the nature center another day. It has some interesting items you'll want to see. There is so much to do here. That's Sieur de Monts Springs inside that small structure there with the octagonal roof. It was built by George Dorr in 1909," Arthur said pointing to the right of the path.

We stopped at a nearby rock engraved with the words "The Sweet Waters of Acadia."

"George Dorr had this stone carved with that phrase to draw attention to the spring. It really brings home the passion that he and others had to make this a national park."

We continued to follow Arthur along the path.

"This area was once the main gathering spot in Acadia when George Dorr served as the first superintendent in 1919."

"So, Mr. Dorr not only helped create the park, he was the park superintendent, too?" I asked.

"He was a high-energy jack-of-all trades, by all accounts," Captain George explained.

"Over there is a Wabanaki wigwam," Arthur explained as he pointed to the left of the path.

Hug-a-Bug, Sarah, Arthur, and I walked over to the wigwam. A sign posted next to it explained that the wigwam is an authentic exhibit built by Penobscot artist, Barry Dana in August 2011. It was refurbished by Passamaquoddy artist, David Moses Bridges, in July 2015.

"The Wabanaki used birch bark to make these wigwams. They could easily assemble them by weaving birch bark sheets between these poles. They would put a firepit in the center and cover the ground inside the wigwam with animal hides," Sarah explained as we stepped inside and sat down. Captain George and Papa Lewis joined us and took a seat.

"Before Europeans settled into this area in the early 1600's, the Wabanaki people would freely navigate the lakeshores and the coastline in birchbark canoes and set up seasonal villages. They were hunters & gatherers," Arthur said, with the confidence of a high school student who has learned about the Wabanaki culture since kindergarten.

We all knew we were about to time travel without a word being said. I looked out the opening to make sure no one was approaching.

"Bubba Jones, take us back to a summer in the early 1600s. The Wabanaki people had some European contact, but the Wabanaki way of life hadn't been fully impacted yet," Captain George said.

"Take us back to the Wabanaki village in July 1610," I said.

Everything went dark, a gust of wind pulled me back, then the light returned. Smoke swirled from glowing embers in the center of the wigwam. We were all dressed in deerskin clothing and sitting on animal hide rugs. We heard chatter in a language we didn't understand outside of the wigwam, and we stepped out to see where we were. The nature center, sidewalk and parking lot were gone. Just thick forest surrounded a camp of wigwams. Several Wabanaki people, dressed in deerskin clothing were busy going about their day. An elderly woman picked up a clay vessel full of clams, brought them over to the fire and set them over the embers. Several men walked into camp carrying a birch bark canoe returning from a day of fishing at sea. Spears and harpoons lay inside the canoe along with a ring of freshly caught fish. A group of women and children returned moments later carrying baskets overflowing with freshly-picked wild berries. A few more men returned to camp from a hunt. They shouldered bows and arrows and carried a stick with a lifeless deer tied to it.

Everyone smiled at us as they walked by, but they continued to go about their activities. The entire camp worked to prepare a meal and sat down and enjoyed it together. Then everyone dispersed to their wigwams. A short while later, all of the Wabanaki people (men, women and children) gathered around a man beating a drum and singing a chant, and everyone began to dance. Some of the men wore headdresses and necklaces.

We didn't converse with anyone since we couldn't speak the language. Our family time travel rule is to observe and learn, minimize contact, and leave no trace or influence. We walked out of the village and found a patch of woods out of view of everyone.

"Wow, the Wabanaki people are amazing. They have it down to a science how to survive out here," Hug-a-Bug whispered.

No one saw the person, who took Arthur's time travel watch. So, we formed a close circle to prepare to time travel back to the present.

"Take us back to the present," I said.

The sky went dark, a gust of wind blew, and then it was light again. We were back in the wigwam near the Abbe Museum.

"What you just saw was just a glimpse of the Wabanaki going about their daily routine in the past. There is so much more to learn about their culture and heritage that you did not get from that time travel experience. I think you'll have a better understanding of their culture after visiting the Abbe museums," Captain George explained.

With that piece of advice, we filed out of the wigwam and back onto the path and soon stood at the entrance to the Abbe Museum, a cement one-story structure with a ceramic tile roof.

"According to the Abbe museum website, this museum is on the National Register of Historic Places. It's one of the last remaining trailside museums. It has over 50,000 artifacts. It's set up similar to the way it was in the 1920's. The Abbe Museum is affiliated with the Smithsonian and their mission is to inspire new learning about the Wabanaki Nations. The Abbe Museum has a modern, second location in Bar Harbor where the Wabanaki people share their own stories, history and culture. We'll visit the Bar Harbor location after this," Captain George explained.

"This location opened in 1928. Dr. Robert Abbe, a plastic surgeon and pioneer in the field of treating cancer using radiation, spent his summers in Bar Harbor. He was deeply interested in the Wabanaki artifacts that were being discovered through archaeological digs on the Mount Desert Island. He started a collection of these artifacts, and with the help of George Dorr, he created a trailside museum to house these artifacts to help piece together the past and learn more about the native people," Captain George continued to explain.

We stepped inside, and an attendant sat just inside

the door. There was a small fee, but Captain George used his family membership to get us all in.

The building felt like it was just as Dr. Abbe left it in 1928. It had a small foyer that opened into a spacious room with high ceilings. Glass display cases lined the walls, filled with tools made from bone and stone, arrow heads, axe heads, harpoons, and fragments of clay pots. There was a description of each item in the case, along with detailed information about how the Wabanaki people lived. Murals on the walls depicted scenes of tribal life, with narratives alongside to explain the Wabanaki history. Having just time traveled to an actual Wabanaki village, it was so cool to see the artifacts from their culture preserved!

"Let's go meet Dr. Abbe," Arthur suggested in a whisper.

"Take us back to the summer of 1927, a year before the Abbe Museum first opened," Captain George suggested.

We slipped out of the building and around the corner. We formed a circle and I said, "Take us back to July 1927."

Everything went dark, a gust of wind blew, and then everything was light again. The Abbe Museum looked like it had just been built. Our clothing had transformed. We all wore formal outfits. The girls wore long dresses and us males wore long pants, collared shirts, and ties. The landscape around the outside of the building was bare. It looked as if a fresh coat of paint had just been applied to the building. We stepped back inside. A well-dressed man wearing a white shirt, tie, and jacket, and sporting a handlebar mustache, stood over a glass case examining a stone tool with a magnifying glass. The man looked up from his work as we entered the room.

"Well, hello folks! I'm Robert Abbe. Welcome," the man greeted us.

"It is an honor to meet you, Dr. Abbe. I admire your work. I hope to become an archeologist one day," Arthur said.

"Thank you! Follow your dream to become an archeologist. My hope is that these archeological discoveries will help solve historical mysteries about how the Wabanaki people lived hundreds and even thousands of years ago. They were the first to settle here. We've collected artifacts that go back 12,000 years. Take your time looking around, and I do hope you enjoy the exhibits on display. Consider yourselves lucky, this museum will not open to the public until next year," Dr. Abbe said.

"Thank you, Dr. Abbe," Captain George replied.

We took some time to explore the exhibits and read the historical descriptions, then thanked Dr. Abbe for sharing these amazing discoveries, and exited the museum. We stepped around to the side of the building, out of sight of everyone and gathered in a circle.

"Did anyone happen to see the boy who took my watch?" Arthur asked, as we stood ready to travel back. We all shook our heads no.

"Take us back to the present," I said, with my hand on the journal in my pocket.

Everything went dark, a gust of wind blew, and when the light hit my eyes, we stood alongside the Abbe Museum in the present day. We were all dressed back in our own outfits.

"Let's head over to the Abbe Museum in Bar Harbor, it's my favorite museum," Sarah said as we followed her along the path back towards the bus stop.

In minutes, we were back on board the Island Explorer. We exited the bus in the center of Bar Harbor and quickly strolled along the sidewalk and around the corner, onto Mt. Desert Street, following Arthur and Sarah. In a few minutes, we stood in front of the Abbe Museum.

For the remainder of the afternoon, we explored the museum. There is a powerful connection, when you learn facts, stories and history from the primary source. Most everything here was a Wabanaki archaeological artifact or an item created by a Wabanaki artist. Arthur showed us the circular room created under the advisement of the Wabanaki people. This room emphasized how important the circle is to the entire Wabanaki way of life. The traditional Penobscot calendar is a circle of the seasons. Circles are an important symbol in Wabanaki art too. Sarah led us around and showed us some of the art and baskets created by the Wabanaki and the traditional clothing. I spent some time reading along a historical timeline. I learned how archaeologists gather clues to learn about people in the past. I could see why Arthur is so interested in archeology. I enjoyed the traditional Wabanaki birchbark canoe that was on display. We all read stories told by tribe members. I learned that unlike other tribes in the United States, the Wabanaki were never removed from there ancestral land. But, they have had to adapt to survive the arrival of Europeans. Today, the Wabanaki people continue to strive to maintain their language, culture, and way of life.

When Captain George told us that it was time to go, there were still several exhibits that Hug-a-Bug and I had not yet seen, but we knew we could come back another day.

As we gathered outside of the museum, Sarah pulled out her wooden hiking stick that was attached to her daypack.

"During one of our lessons in school, we learned that talking sticks are common across many in native American Indian cultures to give everyone a voice. The idea is that everyone has something to contribute and should be allowed to speak. We learned that sharing is a big aspect of the Wabanaki community. My teacher adopted the talking stick for discussions in class to practice good turn taking skills and to give everyone a chance to speak. I thought we could each share what impacted us the most from what we learned about the Wabanaki people today. We'll pass my hiking stick around and when you get the stick, it's your turn to share. I'll go first," Sarah said.

"The creativity of the Wabanaki baskets are amazing," Sarah said as she passed the hiking stick to Arthur.

"I love the circular Penobscot calendar. It makes sense how it connects with the seasons," Arthur said as he passed the hiking stick to Captain George.

"I admire the strength of the Wabanaki people and

how they have endured so much and continue to maintain their community and heritage," Captain George said as he passed the stick to Hug-a-Bug.

"I enjoyed reading the stories told by the tribe members," Hug-a-Bug said as she passed the hiking stick to me.

"When I came across the birchbark canoe exhibit, all of the sudden I was paddling along the ocean shore and the boat was bobbing with the powerful ocean waves. I could feel a gentle cool breeze. For a split second, I thought we had time traveled. That's the sign of a well-done museum, when you feel the experience inside you," I said as I handed the hiking stick to my dad.

"I'm sad to learn of the hardships the Wabanaki people have had to deal with due to colonization and continue to deal with today," Dad said as he passed the hiking stick to Papa Lewis.

"I'm glad that the Wabanaki people remain an active part of the community. I hope that our family mission of preserving and protecting our natural wildlands will help preserve the ancestral lands of the Wabanaki people," Papa Lewis said as he handed the hiking stick back to Sarah.

CHAPTER 8

LOBSTER, BLUEBERRIES, AND FAMILY, OH MY!

"So, we haven't seen the watch thief since our visit to George Dorr's home, and we've time traveled to two significant points in park history. Should we keep exploring the park this way?" Arthur asked his dad.

"I think so. It's the best chance we've got at running into that boy again. We had better get back for dinner. It's getting late. We can plan the rest of our adventure over some lobster," Captain George said.

"Lobster? Yum!" Hug-a-Bug replied.

"Maine lobster is the best there is, and it's caught fresh right here," Arthur answered.

"The more we learn about Acadia and Mount Desert Island, the easier it will be to get your watch back," I responded.

We regrouped at the bus stop. Soon, the Island Explorer slowed to a stop, opened its doors, and we all boarded for a short ride back to Bar Harbor. We arrived in minutes, filed off the bus, and walked a short distance back to our Maine clan's home. As we approached the house, Fran met us in the yard.

"We're going to eat on the back deck. We're having a traditional lobster bake. We bought some lobster and clams fresh off the boat down at the dock. I hope you're all hungry," Fran said.

"I've never had a lobster bake before," I said.

"You're kidding! Boy, are you in for a treat! Lobster is big business here in Maine. I've been eating it for dinner since I was a little kid, and I never grow tired of it," Arthur said.

We all gathered around the table. Fran brought out plates of steamed clams with little cups of melted butter to dip the meat in as a snack before dinner. Everyone helped themselves. We filled Fran, Grandma, and Mom in on our time-travel adventures, adding that we hadn't run into the boy who stole Arthur's watch.

"I like Captain George's plan to explore all the historical sites in the park. It's probably the best chance we've got at getting that watch back," Papa Lewis said.

Fran, Grandma, and Mom disappeared into the house, and reemerged with the main course. They set before each of us a plate with a giant red lobster in the center, surrounded by corn on the cob, coleslaw, and red potatoes. We bowed our heads, and Captain George led us in a dinner prayer.

He ended the prayer by saying, "...and let's pray we get our time-travel watch back." Everyone said amen.

Arthur and Sarah showed Hug-a-Bug and me how to crack open the lobster claws and how to dig the lobster meat out of the tail.

"This was the most unbelievable meal I have ever eaten," I said after I cleaned my plate.

"Save room! We're not done yet! Here's dessert," Fran said as she handed everyone a slice of Maine blueberry cobbler.

"We'll eat some more lobster while you're here; you're in lobster country. Before this adventure is over, we'll take you behind the scenes of the lobster industry," Captain George said to all of us.

"The ocean that surrounds Mount Desert Island is as much a part of Acadia National Park as the land. Not only should we explore the ocean as part of our adventure, it might help us solve the mystery of the missing watch," Papa Lewis said.

After dinner, Hug-a-Bug and I followed Sarah and Arthur inside to what they called the map room. The walls were covered with large maps of the area, nautical charts, and pictures of Acadia. We sat down around a table to look over maps, charts, and guidebooks of Acadia National Park to plan our next day of adventure, with hopes of retrieving the missing time-travel watch.

Arthur and Sarah both suggested that we hike along a few of their favorite trails the next day. They used the word "epic," and they hooked us when they said we would end our adventure at the beach. We all agreed that mountains and beaches were a great combination! The plan was set. We joined Fran, Captain George, Papa Lewis, Grandma, Dad and Mom in the backyard around the fire. They were reminiscing about adventures gone by.

"What did you come up with?" Captain George asked us as we sat down around a crackling fire.

"We're going to take the Jones clan on the Gorham Loop hike. We will walk by Thunder Hole and end at Sand Beach," Arthur explained.

"I think that's a great idea. That is one of the most popular areas in the park, and you will see why tomorrow. We should all get a good night's rest so we can hit the trail early. The best way to catch up to the boy who has our watch is to keep visiting the highlights of Acadia National Park. The more we tour, the more opportunity we will have to run into him," Captain George replied.

On that note, everyone stood and exchanged good-nights. Captain George grabbed a fireplace poker and separated the logs, which reduced the flames to glowing embers within the fire pit, and then he doused it all with a bucket of water. We all headed into the house to our sleeping quarters.

As I lay in my sleeping bag on the floor of Arthur's room, I wondered to myself if simply visiting the highlights of Acadia would be enough to get that time travel watch back. I didn't want to disappoint our Maine clan. They asked us to come here because of our reputation for solving mysteries. My thoughts whirled around what more we could do as I drifted off to sleep.

The smell of bacon awakened me. The sun filtered through the window shade. The clock on Arthur's nightstand read 7:15 a.m. This was the latest I had slept since we arrived on Mount Desert Island. I sat up and slipped into my adventure clothes. Arthur was already up and out of the bedroom. I followed the smell of bacon all the way to the kitchen. The room was buzzing with activity.

"Good morning, Bubba Jones. Did you sleep well?" Fran asked as she looked over her shoulder at me, taking her eyes briefly off the bacon sizzling in the skillet.

"You bet! Thank you," I replied.

"Morning, Bubba," Mom said as she pulled a piece of toast out of the toaster and spread butter on it.

"Breakfast will be ready soon. Everyone else is in the map room going over the plan for the day," Fran stated.

"Great! Thank you," I replied.

Grandma sat quietly at the kitchen table packing our lunch for the day.

"Morning, Grandma," I said.

"Good morning, Bubba Jones," she replied.

I walked out of the kitchen, through the dining room and living room, into the map room. Captain George,

Papa Lewis, Arthur, Sarah, and Hug-a-Bug sat around the table with maps unfolded.

"Good morning, Bubba Jones. You're just in time for the morning briefing," Captain George said.

"That sounds like something you would say if you were in the military," I said as I sat down at the table.

"Sorry, I don't mean to sound so military, but after twenty-two years of service, it's ingrained in me," Captain George responded.

"Where did you serve?" I asked.

"I served in the U.S. Navy, stationed right here, not far from Bar Harbor, but that's another story. Lewis, that reminds me, I need to talk with you in private about something later," Captain George replied.

"Sounds good," Papa Lewis replied.

"There are over 130 miles of hiking trails on Mount Desert Island, but the park does not allow overnight backpacking. We're going to take you on one of our favorite day hikes. Arthur and Sarah will explain the details," Captain George said.

Arthur placed his index finger on the map between the words "Sand Beach" and "Beehive" and said, "We will catch the Island Explorer from Bar Harbor to the Sand Beach upper parking lot here. From there, we will walk along the Ocean Path, up onto Gorham Mountain Trail, and then back down to Sand Beach. The loop is about four miles."

"This hike is ranked as moderate in difficulty, so everyone in our clan should be able to do it. Best of all, after the hike, we can all enjoy Sand Beach," Sarah explained.

"Yes! The beach!" Hug-a-Bug said excitedly.

"Breakfast is ready," Fran hollered from the kitchen.

"We'll assemble our packs after breakfast. We need to make sure everyone is up for this," Captain George said.

We all stood up and headed towards the kitchen. Grandma had finished packing our trail lunches, and the center of the kitchen table was loaded down with a platter of crisp bacon, a big bowl of scrambled eggs, a jar of fresh Maine blueberry jam, a plate of buttered toast, and pitchers of orange juice and milk. Everyone sat down and dug in. Papa Lewis and Captain George discussed the trail with Grandma to see if she was up for it. Grandma has some knee issues. She smiled and said, "I love that hike. It's been a long time. Count me in!"

After breakfast, Papa Lewis and Captain George stepped outside to have a private conversation. I could see Captain George gesturing with his hands. Based on the looks on their faces, they were discussing something serious. This must be the conversation Captain George had mentioned earlier, when he said he needed to speak in private with Papa Lewis. Papa Lewis wrote something down on a piece of paper and slipped it into his shirt pocket. I wondered what was going on, but it was none of my business, so I went back to the map room to help everyone pack up. Each of us packed full water containers and the lunch that Grandma made.

"Cadillac," Arthur called.

The dog jumped up from underneath the table. His tail wagged in excitement when he saw that Arthur had a saddlebag to strap on him. Cadillac stood still while Arthur clipped the saddlebag onto his back. You could tell that the dog was used to carrying this bag.

"He carries his own food and water. He's been on this hike many times," Arthur explained.

Cadillac positioned himself next to the front door, ready to go. The ten of us marched down to the village green led by Cadillac, hopped onto the Sand Beach Island Explorer, and were off.

CHAPTER 9

Mountain Magic

The bus entered the park and pulled onto Park Loop Road. In minutes, we pulled into a parking lot bustling with tourists. We all stepped off the bus and into the crowd. Arthur clipped a leash onto Cadillac. He was so well-trained that he wouldn't need the leash, but park rules required it.

Everyone was ready to hike, so Sarah, Arthur, and Cadillac led us up towards Park Loop Road and onto the Ocean Path. In minutes, we emerged out of the tree canopy with a stunning view of the Atlantic Ocean on our left. A cool ocean breeze blew through my hair.

We could hear distant waves rhythmically crash onto the rocky shoreline. The amazing view made it easy to forget that we were walking alongside a busy road amid a throng of tourists.

"This path is one of many projects completed by the Civilian Conservation Corps, or the CCC as it came to be called, Roosevelt's Tree Army. President Franklin Delano Roosevelt created the CCC as part of his New Deal to help America during the Great Depression. Thousands of people were without work. Businesses were closed, and people were starving. FDR put men to work in the CCC and many of the projects were centered around building our national parks. It not only gave the workers an income; it gave them a sense of pride, and it taught thousands of young men new skills. The CCC boys were fed three meals a day and paid $30.00 a month. All but $5.00 was sent home to their families. The camps were run by the Army but the work was supervised by the National Park Service. Here in Acadia, the CCC had two camps. They built the campgrounds and many of the trails. The Ocean Path was one of their prized projects," Captain George explained.

"Are you thinking what I'm thinking?" Hug-a-Bug said, looking at me.

"Yeah, we've met these CCC workers in other parks. Let's check them out here in Acadia," I replied.

We all climbed off the Ocean Path, ducked behind some bushes, and huddled together. I placed my hand on the family journal.

"This is the first time I've time traveled with a dog. Here it goes," I said.

"Cadillac will be just fine," Arthur assured us.

"Take us back to June 1934," I said.

Everything went dark. A gust of wind hit us and then it was light again. We stepped out from behind the bushes, and now it was an entirely different scene. Army trucks were parked on a gravel road, and hundreds of young men dressed in army green uniforms were busy at work. A team of men wedged logs beneath a huge boulder to lever it into place along the Ocean Path. They were dripping with sweat. All along the shore, small groups of men were moving rocks into place that weighed thousands of pounds, to build the Ocean Path. Other work teams planted trees. We scrutinized the various groups of workers in hopes of finding the boy who took Arthur and Sarah's watch. He was nowhere in sight.

"They definitely earned their $30.00 a month," I whispered.

"In the 1930s, $30.00 could feed and clothe a small family for a month, with money to spare," Papa Lewis whispered.

A man in a park ranger's hat, who had moments ago barked out orders to the CCC workers, walked toward us.

"Hello there! Pardon our construction. But when these men are done you will have a much better path to walk along as you enjoy this fabulous seashore. Enjoy your visit," the national park official said.

"I'm confident this path will be used by many to enjoy

Acadia National Park. Thank you," Captain George replied.

The national park official tipped his hat to us, and walked back toward a group of men and directed them where to place another large boulder. We slipped behind some nearby bushes. I placed my hand on the family journal and said, "Take us back to the present."

The sky went dark, a gust of wind pressed against me, and then the sky lit up again. We stepped back onto the Ocean Path and continued our walk. In a short while, we reached a sign announcing Thunder Hole. A staircase led us down off the Ocean Path to the site. We mingled with a crowd of onlookers to see this small cavern leading off the ocean. Waves crashed through the narrow rock wall and smacked into the cavern. It made a thunderous crash, hence the name: Thunder Hole.

"Depending on the weather and tide, sometimes it's too dangerous to stand down here. The waves completely cover the stairs," Captain George said.

We watched the waves crash into Thunder Hole, and we took some pictures. This was so cool! It was easy to see why so many people were here to watch these massive waves make impact. Eventually, we all walked back up the stairs and onto the Ocean Path. The coast was lush with spruce trees, dogwoods, and other foliage. We passed by Monument Cove, a small rock-strewn beach.

"Just south of here are the Otter Cliffs and Otter Point. We'll come back to explore those another time," Arthur stated as we crossed the Park Loop Road to reach the foot of the Gorham Mountain Trail. Arthur stopped at the trailhead and pulled a collapsible bowl and water bottle out of Cadillac's saddlebag. He poured some water in the bowl and placed it on the ground for Cadillac to drink. Sarah pulled off her daypack and retrieved a canister of insect repellant.

"Everyone should put some of this on before we get into the woods. There are plenty of mosquitoes and ticks out here. Black fly season is over, thank goodness. Those can be bothersome, too," Sarah said as she misted the spray on her exposed skin and then passed the can to me.

We filed up the Gorham Mountain Trail with Cadillac in the lead. Once we left the flat and easy Ocean Path Trail, we also left behind the crowds. So far, we had the trail all to ourselves. Grandma's knees were bothering her, so we stopped to let her rest and assured her that whenever she needed a break, to just let us know. Grandma's rest break allowed all of us to catch our breath on the ascent. Just after Grandma alerted us that she would like to take another rest, we rounded a bend in the trail and noticed a plaque embedded into the side of the granite mountain. It was a perfect spot for a break, with room for everyone to sit on a flat rock to rest. The plaque was about 12 inches by 18 inches and it read: "Waldron Bates Memoriam 1856-1908, Pathmaker."

"Who was Waldron Bates?" I asked as we all sat drinking from our water bottles.

"He blazed most of the hiking trails here in Acadia. Do you see that small stack of rocks?" Arthur asked, pointing to a neatly-stacked pile of rocks nearby.

The stack had two base rocks weighted down with one large rock placed over them and then a smaller rock perched on top.

"That's called a Bates cairn, named after Waldron Bates. Cairns are used to mark trails. They are especially useful when there are no trees to post trail markers on. Mr. Bates designed his own type of cairn," Arthur explained.

"So that is why he's known as 'the Pathmaker.' He had

a trail name before trail names were popular, just like hikers get on the Appalachian Trail. That's cool. I would like to meet 'the Pathmaker,'" I responded.

"Take us back to a summer between 1900 and 1909. Mr. Bates was chairman of the Bar Harbor Path Committee and he was busy making trails during that time period," Captain George responded.

Everyone moved in close to me. I grabbed hold of the family journal and said, "Take us back to June 21st, 1905."

Everything went dark, a gust of wind pushed against me, then it was light again. Our hiking clothes were replaced with old-fashioned dress clothes. The ladies wore dresses down to their ankles with wide brim sun hats, and the menfolk wore long pants, white shirts with bow ties, suit coats, and wide brim hats. We were a bit overdressed, in my opinion, for a hike in the woods, and the clothes felt too warm for the season. A group of men walked by, each of them carrying a large rock on their shoulders as they headed up Gorham Mountain. Beads of sweat rolled down their faces. I looked carefully at each person, in search of the boy who took Arthur and Sarah's watch. No luck. A man dressed in a suit like mine walked down the trail from the direction of the Gorham Mountain summit. He stopped and made some notes on what looked like a hand-drawn map. When he noticed us, he stopped and introduced himself.

"Well, hello! I'm Waldron Bates. They call me the Pathmaker. I'm so glad you chose this trail. It's one of my favorites. It's good to get out here and enjoy nature. We've almost completed placement of the cairns," Mr. Bates said.

"Mr. Pathmaker, what is the little rock on top of the cairn for?" I asked, pointing at the Bates cairn nearby where we sat.

"Magnificent question, young man. I designed these cairns so they are big enough to see, but small enough so as not to take up too much space or interfere with the view. The top rock points in the direction of the trail so you know where to walk. I'm on the Bar Harbor Path Committee, and we're placing cairns along the trails in the park. I'm also drawing up maps for everyone to use. Enjoy your hike. You shouldn't get lost if you follow the cairns," Mr. Bates answered as he walked on.

Soon, the coast was clear to travel back to the present without being seen. Everyone stood up and circled together. I clutched the family journal and said, "Take us back to the present."

Everything went dark, a gust of wind hit me, and then it was light again. We were all back in our hiking clothes, and I caught a whiff our bug repellant.

"Now that was cool! We met the Pathmaker!" Hug-a-Bug said with a grin.

We continued up the mountain in single file. An occasional group of hikers passed us, going down the mountain, but the number of people we encountered was minimal compared to the Ocean Path. Whenever Grandma needed a break, we followed Arthur and Sarah to some nearby bushes to pick wild blueberries, eating the plump, ripe berries on the spot. Mmm-mmm! We continued following blue trail markers and Bates Cairns all the way to the Gorham Mountain summit. Grandma was relieved when she saw the summit sign perched above a pile of rocks. The sign indicated an elevation of 525 feet; not that high as far as mountains go, but a gentle breeze blew in off the ocean, and it felt good to be at the top. We stood on a massive boulder high above the tree line, and took in the view. We could see out to Frenchman Bay, and beyond that, some islands in the distance. To our left, I spotted Sand Beach, where we planned to end our hike, and just beyond Sand Beach was another area identified on the map as Great Head. Trees and shrubs struggled to survive up here due to the harsh weather conditions. We all sat down and brought out the lunch that Grandma had packed for us. Arthur filled Cadillac's water bowl and pulled out some dog food for him. Cadillac lapped up the water, ate his food, and then sat down next to us.

"Cadillac sure is a good dog," I said.

"Yeah, he loves it out here," Arthur replied.

This sure was the life! For a little while, we all sat chatting, laughing, and enjoying the day as if we didn't have a care in the world. We all seemed to completely forget about the missing time travel watch. We were under the wonderful spell of Acadia, relaxed and at peace, surrounded by the beauty of nature.

After everyone finished lunch, we snapped some family pictures, then shouldered our packs and headed down the trail toward Sand Beach.

CHAPTER 10

BEACH WATCH

We continued along Gorham Mountain Trail, down the mountain, following the Bates cairns and the blue blazes. We had to go extra slow to keep Grandma from injuring her sore knees. Most falls and injuries happen when you're hiking downhill. We came upon a trail junction and got out the maps. Two trails split off, one going to the Bowl and the other going to the Beehive.

"We'll come back and hike the Beehive another time if anyone is interested, but it's too difficult for Grandma, and we can't take Cadillac. The Bowl is a great pond for swimming, but for today, we'll stick to Sand Beach," Arthur said.

We all followed Cadillac down the mountain and crossed the Park Loop Road, returning to where we had started in the Sand Beach parking lot.

"That was a great hike. It had everything: views, history, blueberries, and now the beach!" Hug-a-Bug exclaimed with excitement.

I smiled and nodded in agreement, trying to hide my disappointment that we had not encountered the watch thief. After all, that's why we were dispatched here.

"Sometimes when you follow a strategy, like we're doing to get that time-travel watch back, it requires patience, like casting a fishing line and waiting for a fish. Never underestimate the power of a relaxing time on a beach. Let's go," Captain George said.

Wow, Captain George seemed to read my mind, just like Papa Lewis! Those two are two peas in a pod, that's for sure.

"I'll take Cadillac for a stroll while you enjoy Sand Beach," Fran offered.

"Dogs aren't allowed at Sand Beach," Sarah explained.

We walked down a set of stairs to the beach. Sand Beach is in a little cove off the ocean. It is sheltered on both sides by rocky cliffs. It looked like a vacation paradise with white sand, a lifeguard perched up on the lifeguard post, and tourists lying on towels under beach umbrellas. Mom pulled some towels from her backpack and we all sat down in the sun.

"Let's go for a swim," Hug-a-Bug eagerly suggested as she took off her hiking shoes and socks.

"There are a few things you should know about this beach. It's the only ocean beach with sand in Acadia, and the sand is made of ground-up sea shells mixed with rock particles. The powerful waves hitting the rocky shoreline over time pulverized the sea shells and gradually ground down the rocks over time. The water is too cold for swimming; it's only about 55 degrees," Captain George explained.

When you tell a kid that water is too cold to swim in, it becomes a challenge. Hug-a-Bug, Arthur, Sarah, and I waded into the ocean, and just like Captain George said, the water was freezing. We splashed around in the waves for a little bit until the cool water became unbearable, and then we returned to the beach to dry off and warm up.

"We can go swimming another day at Echo Lake. The water's much warmer there," Arthur said.

We all sat on our towels and relaxed, and enjoyed the great weather and picturesque view. Then, the unbelievable happened. The boy that we'd been looking for sat on a towel by himself, about twenty yards in front of us, staring out toward the water.

"Hey guys, don't get up or say anything, but the watch thief we've been looking for is sitting on a blue towel twenty yards in front of us. I don't believe he saw us," I said quietly.

"Let's get him," Arthur whispered.

"No, wait! I think Hug-a-Bug and I should follow him. He doesn't know we're with you guys, so if he sees us, he shouldn't be alarmed. He might be startled if he recognizes us from one of our time-travel adventures, but he won't view us as a threat like he would you. You're the one who tried to take back the time-travel pocket watch," I whispered back.

"That's a good idea, Bubba Jones. You, Hug-a-Bug, Grandma, Petunia, Clark, and I will separate from the the rest of our group right now. We can all meet back at the house later," Papa Lewis whispered.

"I'll go tell Fran what's going on," Captain George whispered.

Hug-a-Bug, Grandma, my parents, and I followed Papa Lewis further down the beach away from Arthur and Sarah's family, but still within sight of the boy. We spread out our towels and sat on the sand.

"We'll stay here until he leaves. Then we'll follow him at a distance and hope he doesn't realize he's being followed," Papa Lewis said.

We watched from afar for several minutes, like detectives. Then the boy stood up, rolled up his towel, tucked it under his arm, threw a backpack over his shoulder, and walked toward the stairs leading up to the parking lot. I did not see the time-travel watch. We all stood up, quickly rolled up our towels and followed him, keeping a good distance so he wouldn't notice us. Grandma's knees started to act up again as we climbed the steps up to the parking lot. We stopped to see if she was okay.

"I'm fine," Grandma whispered to us.

While we stopped for those few seconds, the boy reached the top of the stairs and disappeared. Hug-a-Bug, Papa Lewis, and I left Grandma with Dad and Mom and ran up the steps to get a visual on the boy. But when we reached the top of the stairs, he was nowhere in sight. An Island Explorer bus full of people pulled away from the bus stop. We walked over and sat on a bench by the bus stop and watched to see if the boy simply went to the restroom or one of the changing rooms. Minutes went by, and we didn't see him. Grandma, Mom, and Dad caught up to us and sat down. The boy could have ridden off on the bus, drove off in a car, or he went on a hike.

Even though we lost him, this was the boost we needed to keep searching. Just when I felt like the trail had grown cold with no sightings of the pocket watch thief, we discovered him again. Not only that, it was in the present, not during a time-travel episode. Captain George's idea of simply exploring the park had worked. This assured me that if we kept exploring, we would run into him soon again. Now, all we needed to do was devise a way to get that watch back.

A distant mountain with a rounded top perched above the trees off in the distance, behind Sand Beach. It had caught my attention earlier from the Beach, and it grabbed my attention again from the parking lot. I glanced at my map and found it: the Beehive. That was the trail we didn't hike earlier because of Grandma's knees. I wondered if the boy went up that mountain when we lost him. I remembered a conversation Arthur had with me about the trail to the Beehive being a difficult hike. I decided it would not be a good idea to go looking for the boy on the Beehive Trail without my cousins. But my curiosity was piqued. I wanted to go up that mountain.

We gave up looking for the watch thief and caught the Island Explorer back to Bar Harbor. When we stepped off the bus, I stopped and huddled everyone together.

"We should walk past our cousins' home to make sure that the boy didn't follow us. We don't want to give away our family connection," I suggested.

"Very good idea, Bubba Jones. I was going to suggest that same thing. You're a natural sleuth," Papa Lewis said.

We marched towards our cousins' home, but instead of walking up to the door, we continued along the sidewalk, past their house, and around the corner onto a side street. Then we turned around and walked back towards the house to see if anyone had followed us. The coast was clear; no one was in sight. So we returned to their home and let ourselves in using the key they had given us. They were all sitting in the living room when we stepped through the door.

"Well, what happened? Did you track the boy?" Arthur blurted as soon as we stepped inside and shut the front door.

"Yes, but we lost him in the Sand Beach parking lot. The good news is we know we can track him in the present, not just in the past. He's either a tourist or a resident, and he's somewhere on Mount Desert Island right now. Captain George's idea of exploring all of Acadia's highlights worked. We need to keep exploring Acadia and continue our efforts to find that boy. The more encounters we have with him, the more we learn about his habits, and the better our chances will be to get that watch back," I said.

"Excellent point, Bubba Jones. We'll stick to our adventure agenda, then," Captain George said.

"We have a few hours before dinner. Just enough time to do some tide pooling and kayaking," Arthur said.

"What's tide pooling?" Hug-a-Bug asked.

"Well, let's go down to Bar Island, and we'll show you. It's just a short walk, and it's low tide right now," Arthur said.

Hug-a-Bug, Sarah, and I stood to join Arthur. Our parents were lost in conversation, and it didn't look like they were interested or had the energy to come along, but Papa Lewis stood up with a grin on his face.

"I love tide pooling and kayaking. Can I join you?" he asked.

"Sure, Papa Lewis," Arthur responded.

"Okay, you can come along too, Cadillac," Arthur said.

Cadillac wagged his tail in excitement and danced in circles by the door. We filed out onto the front porch. Cadillac was so smart and well-trained. He knew from our conversation where to go. He led us along the sidewalk and through neighborhoods lined with old, well-kept homes. Many of the homes had been converted to inns and bed and breakfasts. We cut over onto West

Street and then turned onto Bridge Street, which led us down the road and out to the ocean. A small forested island came into view just off the coast, and a sandbar allowed passage all the way across the water to the Island. There were people walking along the sandbar out to the island. Arthur and Sarah led us out onto the sandbar. Cadillac took off in a sprint and left us in his dust.

"He loves low tide on this sandbar," Sarah explained.

"This is the Bar Island Trail. It's usually under water except during low tide. We've got about two hours before the tide comes back in. This is a great place to go tide pooling. There are living organisms that can survive in two climates, under water and above water, during low tide. These organisms have evolved to survive drastic change, going from being submerged under the sea water, to being exposed to air," Arthur said.

"There are three levels of intertidal zones: high, mid, and low. Different species thrive in each zone. We'll look around and try to find some examples of the species in each zone," Sarah explained.

"Wow, you guys are loaded with fun facts," Hug-a-Bug said.

"The Dorr Museum of Natural History, on the campus of the College of the Atlantic here in town, has some great programs about the park and the sea life. Our parents have taken us there since we were little. We've explored all the exhibits, and have even taken some summer classes," Sarah replied.

"Ah yes, your grandmother and I visited the College

of the Atlantic the last time we were here. The museum building is the original headquarters of Acadia National Park," Papa Lewis added.

"The museum has an indoor tidepool that they've created so you can learn all about tide pooling. They also have some cool artifacts. You can learn all about whales, too," Arthur said.

Sarah and Arthur pointed out barnacles, tiny white shells stuck to the exposed rocks along the rocky shore. They explained that the barnacles live in the high tidal zone, and they close up when out of water. But when they are submerged, they open up and feed off little organisms living in the water called plankton. They showed us snails and explained that the snails can bore a hole into barnacles and eat them. We found sea stars, mussels, and snails, all intertidal sea life, submerged in pools of water between the rocks. They showed us Irish moss and another type of seaweed called rockweed that flourishes in the intertidal zone. Sarah pointed out a sea urchin which looked like a Koosh ball. She explained that sea urchins eat the algae

"Wow, there is a whole food chain going on here in small pools of water!" I stated.

We walked on in search of a sea cucumber, an ugly sea creature shaped like a cucumber.

CHAPTER 11

PADDLES & THIEVES

A kayaker paddled close to us and waved. Arthur, Sarah and the rest of us waved back.

"That looks fun," Hug-a-Bug said looking at the kayaker.

"That's Commodore Don, he owns a kayak and bike rental shop in town. Commodore Don served in the Navy at Winter Harbor with our Dad and he's also one of our cousins. We help in his store, tuning bikes, and cleaning kayaks, and, in turn, he lets us use the kayaks and bikes free of charge. We made plans with him to take us on a short kayak paddle."

"So, he's part of the family?" I asked.

"If you're referring to our time-travel secret, yes. Captain George will fill you in about him later," Arthur explained.

"I haven't seen Don in years," Papa Lewis said.

"Is that Lewis?" Commodore Don shouted.

"Hey, Don. It's been a long time," Papa Lewis replied.

"Captain George briefed me on why you're here," Commodore Don replied.

"Yeah, the missing watch. We're working on it. You would never know we're on a mission with all the fun that we're having," Papa Lewis replied.

"Well, let's do a little exploring around Bar Island. The tide is in our favor right now. I have some extra sea kayaks tied up over by the shore next to the Bar Harbor Club. Let's get everyone into some life jackets. I'll go over the basics and then lead us on a little adventure," Commodore Don explained as he pointed to the kayaks near the shore.

A staff member from Commodore Don's store hollered for Cadillac. The dog turned and ran towards the staff member, who ushered the dog into his truck parked nearby. We all zipped on life vests and Arthur untied our kayaks one by one and helped us into the cockpits. Commodore Don instructed us on how to hold the paddle and steer. We practiced using our hips to roll the kayak and return it to the upright position. Man, that ocean water was cold! When everyone felt comfortable enough with their kayak skills, Commodore Don took the lead and we all paddled over to Bar Island. We steered along the shore and worked our way around to the other side of the island.

"Be on the lookout for seals. They are very common to see along the shores of these islands, which is awesome considering that they were almost completely extinct at one point in history. There are two types, harbor seals and grey seals. Grey seals are the larger of the two and can grow up to eight feet long. Seals like to sun themselves on the rocky seashores. Fishermen used to consider the seals a threat and would kill them because the seals eat the fish, but the Marine Mammal Protection Act was put in place in 1972 to protect seals, whales, dolphins, porpoises, and sea turtles. Since then, the seal population has rebounded. They can be dangerous though. They have sharp teeth, so don't get too close," Commodore Don explained.

We paddled along the Bar Island shore, but we didn't see any seals. Even though it was a hot day, a cool breeze kicked up from the water. The rhythmic paddling and awesome scenery was enjoyable. I started to get the hang of sea kayaking and it was fun.

Then all of the sudden, Commodore Don yelled, "The tide is rising and the waves are getting choppy! Let's head back to shore. We can go out another day when you have more time."

We all followed Commodore Don and turned around and paddled back the way we came. This was a pretty good work out and I was tired from paddling, but we still had some distance to cover before reaching shore. We all stopped paddling for a short break, floating together off shore behind the Bar Island Club. That's when I noticed the boy who took the time-travel watch. He was standing on the pool deck at the Bar Harbor Club. He didn't notice us because he was focused on a book he was reading. Besides that, we all wore wide brimmed hats and sunglasses, so it would be hard to recognize us if he did look up. I paddled up alongside Hug-a-Bug and Papa Lewis.

"Don't look now, but 'the boy' is standing by that pool at the Bar Island Club Resort next to where we're heading. I'm going to race to shore and go up there," I said in a whisper.

"I'll come with you. Hug-a-Bug, you stay back and explain what's happening to Arthur and Sarah," Papa Lewis said.

My adrenaline kicked in. I felt a surge of energy and paddled as fast as I could. Papa Lewis kept up with me and we reached the bank at the same time. We hopped out of our kayaks, being careful to keep them balanced. We unzipped our life vests and quickly walked up Bridge Street, then hung a left onto West Street and walked to the front entrance of the Bar Harbor Club.

"Bubba Jones, this was an exclusive private club for the rich and famous that once owned summer mansions and estates up here. J.P. Morgan built this club in 1929. Joseph Pulitzer, George Vanderbilt, John S. Kennedy, John D. Rockefeller Jr., and many others belonged to this club. They attended fancy parties," Papa Lewis explained.

A plaque to the left of the main entrance confirmed what Papa Lewis was saying. The resort club had changed ownership. It was recently renovated to some of its original luster and is now open once again.

"You mean Pulitzer, as in the Pulitzer Prize, and John D. Rockefeller Jr., the son of the oil man, John D. Rockefeller, the richest man in America?" I asked.

"Yep. This was their summer hideaway nearly a hundred years ago," Papa Lewis confirmed.

"Why is that boy here? Let's try and find out without scaring him off," I said as we opened the door and stepped inside.

As soon as we entered the building, a door attendant greeted us.

"Welcome. Are you members or hotel guests?" the door attendant asked.

"Neither, we just want to have a look around if you don't mind," Papa Lewis answered.

"Are you interested in joining our club?" the attendant asked Papa Lewis.

"Perhaps in the future," Papa Lewis answered.

"Have a look around. I'll be happy to answer any questions," the door attendant said.

Papa Lewis and I walked through the building and out the back door, which led us through a grass court yard. I was afraid we would lose the boy again if we didn't hurry. We walked faster along a sidewalk, down some steps, passed some tennis courts, went through another building, and finally out to the oceanside pool. The boy was still there sitting in a pool side chair, reading a book. We found some chairs across the pool from him and sat down. An attendant approached us.

"Would you like some menus?" she asked.

"Not right now, but can you tell me who that boy is?" Papa Lewis asked.

"His name is Mic, at least that's what his ID said. He's not a boy, he's an adult. I thought he looked rather young, that's why I checked his ID. He's been asking all sorts of questions about the history of the club and its members. Why do you want to know?" the poolside attendant responded.

"He looks familiar. What state is his ID from?" I asked.

"Maine," the attendant answered.

"Thank you," I said.

"I'll check back on you guys," the attendant said as she walked on.

"I'm going to find out what he's reading and see if he has the watch with him," I whispered to Papa Lewis.

I stood up and walked around the pool to the far end, near the boy. I stood at the railing overlooking Bar Island. I could see Commodore Don down below with Hug-a-Bug and our cousins. They were loading the kayaks onto a trailer hitched to Commodore Don's truck. I turned and walked past Mic, trying to blend in like a curious tourist. Mic held a book open in his hands titled, *Bar Harbor: A Town Almost Lost*, and a second book lay next to him on the table. I couldn't read the entire title of the book on the table, but I saw the name "Henry Every" in the title. I also saw the chain of the time-travel pocket watch clipped to his belt loop which led into his front pocket—Mic was definitely the watch thief! My heart throbbed with adrenaline. I wanted to grab the watch from him and run, but there was no way I could do it without a struggle and lots of commotion, and it would be hard to prove that the watch didn't belong to him. Mic didn't pay any attention to me, so my cover was not blown. I walked back over to Papa Lewis and sat down.

As soon as I leaned back in my chair, Mic stood up, placed the books under his arm, and walked toward the door, leaving the pool area. As soon as he stepped through the door into the building, we stood up and followed him. We walked through the building, putting some distance between us. We followed him out a second set of doors, went past the tennis courts, then up the steps and across the grass covered court yard. As soon as he entered the main building, we darted across the court yard, seconds behind him. Mic slipped out of the main entrance door onto West Street just as we entered the building. We walked swiftly towards the door. The attendant stood nearby smiling.

"Well, what did you think? Do you have any questions? We can sit down and go over membership options," the door attendant said as we quickly walked towards the front door.

"We'll have to come back another time—beautiful place you have here," Papa Lewis said, without stopping, as we rushed out the front door.

We stood under a roofed canopy and looked all around for Mic. He was nowhere in sight.

"How did he ditch us? He either time traveled away or ran as soon as he stepped out outside," I said to Papa Lewis.

"You're right, Bubba Jones, but we have some good intelligence on him now," Papa Lewis replied.

CHAPTER 12

MAP IT OUT

Papa Lewis and I walked back to our cousins' house. Everyone was there, including Commodore Don. They all circled around us, excited to hear the details.

As soon as we stepped into the house and shut the front door, we were peppered with questions.

"What happened? Did you get the watch back?" Cousin Arthur asked.

"No, we didn't get the watch, but we learned more information that will help us get it back," I said.

"Like what?" Arthur asked.

"Is there a big space where we can lay out all the

evidence of what we know so far? It might help to think this through, if we can all look at what we've got," I asked.

"Sure, Bubba Jones. How about the map room? We can use the map room as our mission headquarters. There's even a map of the area on the wall," Captain George suggested.

"Perfect," I said as Captain George led me through the house and into the map room.

A large glass framed topographical map of the entire Mount Desert Island and Acadia National Park, including the surrounding ocean and islands, was mounted on the wall. Everyone filed into the map room.

"I'm going to need a few things. Do you have any scotch tape, string, markers, and some paper?" I asked our Maine cousins.

"Coming right up," cousin Sarah responded.

Sarah and Arthur rifled through the drawers of an antique desk that sat in the corner. The desk was from the captain quarters of an old ship. A modern desk top computer perched on the desk. They walked back over to me with all the items that had I requested and set them on the table.

"Do you mind if I write on the glass frame covering the map on the wall? It will wipe right off," I asked Sarah and Arthur.

"Go ahead," Arthur responded.

I took a red marker and drew circles on the glass of the wall map to mark everywhere we had encountered Mic. Then, I drew X's on the map to highlight everywhere else we had been so far without seeing Mic.

Thankfully, Hug-a-Bug keeps a detailed timeline of everywhere we time travel, so she helped me record each Mic encounter, where we've time traveled, and what time period or an exact date we encountered him. We recorded each detail on separate post-it notes. Sarah, Arthur, Hug-a-Bug, and I worked together to record what we had learned and what happened at each separate location. I took the post it notes and stuck them around the map near where each encounter or excursion I had marked on the glass.

"Wow, with all the facts laid out on the wall like that, it looks like a professional police investigation," Commodore Don said.

"Since we can't call the police to report a stolen time-travel watch, this is the next best thing," Arthur responded.

"It also shows that we've barely scratched the surface of exploring MDI and Acadia. Look at all the places we haven't been yet," Hug-a-Bug pointed out.

"We have plenty more adventures to share with you guys. Don't worry about that," Arthur assured us.

"Yeah, we've only just begun," Sarah chimed in.

"We'll keep exploring the island like we've been doing. It looks like we've uncovered some good intelligence. Great work so far, everyone," Captain George said.

"I agree. This is great Bubba Jones, Arthur, Sarah, and Hug-a-Bug," Papa Lewis added.

"Hopefully, this will help us to visually track everything

that's happened and figure out a pattern or clue that will get that time-travel watch back," I said.

"Let's review what we know. The time-travel watch was stolen from Arthur at Mr. Dorr's farm ruins just after you returned from a time travel episode here," I said, using a hiking stick to point to the location on the map.

I continued to review the evidence using the hiking stick as a pointer. "Then we encountered Mic on Cadillac Mountain while time traveling for a ride on the Cog Railway to the Green Mountain House. We encountered Mic again over here at the Jordan Pond House when we time traveled back to taste a popover. We ran into him again when we went back to the ruins of Mr. Dorr's home, the year Acadia officially became a National Monument. Then the trail grew cold. We didn't run into him when we time traveled back and met the Wabanaki natives and Dr. Abbe at the Sieur de Monts Spring area of the park. We didn't see him when we time traveled to meet the CCC as they built the Ocean Path, or when we went back and met Mr. Bates on the Gorham Mountain Trail. Unexpectedly, we encountered him in present time twice, first at Sand Beach, and again the same day at the Bar Harbor Club reading books by the pool.

"So, what do we know about him? We know that he's not a boy, but an adult. He has shown interest in some of the park history, and he likes relaxing at beaches and pools. Based on the books he was reading and the questions he asked the pool attendant, he appears to be interested in the local history. So, what's he after? What

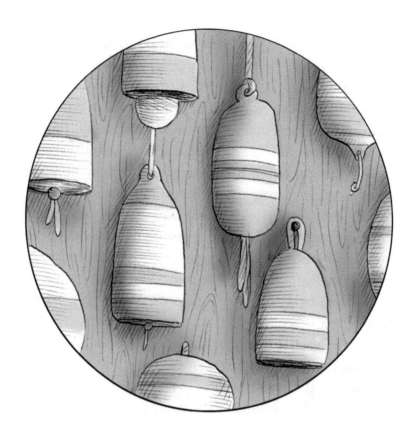

does he want with the time-travel watch and how do we get it back?"

"Wow, you've put this together well. In just two days, look what we've uncovered! I think we should take a break and let this soak in. It's dinner time and Commodore Don would like to treat everyone at his friend's restaurant. It has some of the best food on the island. After dinner, we'll come back and plan our adventure for the next day," Captain George said.

"While we're in public, if we encounter Mic, we need

to separate so he doesn't know we're all working together. In fact, it might be wise to sit at separate tables in the restaurant in case he drops in," I suggested.

"Good advice. You're right Bubba Jones. We don't want to mess up our investigation, so let's walk to and from the restaurant as separate families," Arthur advised.

We left the house in two separate groups, minutes apart from each other. The restaurant was only a few blocks away. Lobster John's was situated on a pier overlooking Frenchman Bay near downtown. The sides of the building were covered with small, football-shaped buoys, each with distinctly different colors and stripes.

"What are those colorful buoys used for?" Hug-a-Bug asked Papa Lewis.

"Those are lobster buoys. Each fisherman has their own unique color and pattern of buoy, and the buoys connect to the lobster traps by a rope. This makes it easy for each fisherman to identify their own traps," Papa Lewis explained.

We entered Lobster John's restaurant and we were led to a table on an outside deck patio. We had a view of the Harbor speckled with fishing boats and sailboats anchored off shore.

"Howdy, folks, I'm Lobstah John. Any friend of Commodore Don is a friend of mine," Lobster John said.

We all said hello.

"This is my restaurant. During the day, I'm on the water catching fish and trapping lobstahs. By night, I'm on land serving up my fresh catch. We have two entrées to choose from tonight, lobstah rolls or lobstah mac. I understand that some of you out-of-townahs haven't had lobstah the way us locals like it. So, let me help you out. A lobstah roll is all the meat from the lobstah shell, mixed with a little mayonnaise, seasoning, a sprinkling of lettuce, chilled for a few minutes, and served on a toasted roll. The work of digging the meat out of the lobstah shell is done for you. Lobstah mac and cheese is perfect for the mac and cheese fans in the group. We've topped the best mac and cheese on the island with the best lobstah in the world, Maine lobstah," Lobster John explained.

A server came around and took everyone's order. A few minutes later, servers approached our table and placed our drinks in front of us and covered the table with delicious looking appetizers, including shrimp cocktail, fried clams, and fried haddock. Lobster John sat down at our table to talk with Commodore Don and Captain George. Arthur explained that they all served together in the Navy.

"I just worked out the details with Commodore Don and Captain George to take you all out on my lobstah boat tomorrow for a tour. Be here on the pier at 8:30 a.m.," Lobster John announced.

"Cool! That will be fun. Thank you!" I said.

"Yeah, that's exciting!" Hug-a-Bug added.

"Lobster John's tour is awesome!" Arthur added.

Dinner arrived and everyone grew quiet while we gobbled down our lobster rolls and lobster mac. Last night, when we ate lobster, I thought that I had the best meal ever. But, this lobster roll was amazing. Hug-a-Bug let me try her lobster mac and it was quite delicious.

We thanked Commodore Don for dinner and Lobster John for a great meal, and then we left in two separate groups and headed back to the house. We all gathered in the map room to make plans for the next day and to review our mission to get the time-travel watch back. We decided that we would all visit the National Park carriage roads after our lobster cruise tomorrow. Everyone was exhausted from our action-packed day, so we all adjourned to our sleeping quarters. I fell asleep as soon as my head hit the pillow.

CHAPTER 13

THE CONNECTION OF LAND & SEA

I woke up to the sweet smell of blueberry pancakes siz-zling in a buttered skillet. The morning sun beamed into the room through the cracks around the window shade. The clock on Arthur's nightstand said 7:00 a.m., yet he was already up and gone and his bed was made. I slipped out of my sleeping bag and followed my nose down to the kitchen. Everyone was assembled at the kitchen table—it was the men's turn to cook this morning. Captain George, Papa Lewis, and Dad placed a platter stacked with warm blueberry pancakes, blueberry syrup, and sausage links on the table, and we all dug in. After breakfast, we applied sunscreen, grabbed our rain parkas, donned hats and sunglasses, and marched down to the pier in two separate groups to meet Lobster John.

"Good morning! Are you ready to go check some pots for bugs? That's slang for checkin' some lobstah traps for lobstah," Lobster John explained.

"You bet," I answered.

"Let's go," Hug-a-Bug added.

Everyone stepped onto Lobster John's boat, then he introduced his three shipmates to us. They each wore bright orange, chest-high, rubber fishing waders held up by beefy suspender straps. He explained that his shipmates would do the fishing and he would navigate and narrate what's going on. His shipmates are all second and third generation lobstermen; they've been catching lobster all their lives. The shipmates untied the boat from the pier and we puttered away out into Frenchman's Bay. The sky was bright and sunny, and even though it was already steamy hot on shore, everyone immediately put their parkas on to keep warm from the cool sea air.

"Before trains and automobiles, the rich and famous, the military, and fisherman came and went to MDI by boat. See that large four-masted schooner sailboat tied to the town pier?" Lobster John asked pointing back towards shore.

"That's the Margaret Todd. They offer narrated sailing excursions," Lobster John explained.

We motored further away from Bar Harbor, and then one of Lobster John's shipmates took the wheel of the boat so Lobster John could talk to us about lobster fishing.

"Many lobstah fishermen make their own traps, also known as a pot. Here's one of mine, which I made from plastic coated wire and netting," Lobster John explained as he held up a four-foot-long rectangle shaped trap.

"There are two rooms in the trap. The first room, called the kitchen, is where the lobstah enters the trap. It crawls up this tunnel of netting and falls into the trap. We hang bait, usually herring, in the trap to lure the lobstah in. Once it's in, it can't get back out the way it entered so it climbs up a second net and into the second room, called the parlor. The trap has a small escape door here in the parlor to allow smaller lobsters to escape. There are strict rules about the size of lobsters we can catch. We're going to pull up some of our traps and see what we have. Our traps are marked by a blue buoy with a white stripe. The buoy is tied to the trap which sits on the ocean floor," Lobster John explained.

The water was sprinkled with an array of different colored buoys bobbing around, each marking a different fisherman's traps. The shipmates reached down and attached an electric pully to one of their blue and white buoys, then one of them hit a switch and the pully wound up the line attached to the trap from the bottom of the sea. They reeled the wet trap up onto the deck. Two lobsters were in the trap and Lobster John pulled one out.

"We always check the underside of the tail. This is where females carry their eggs. If the lobster has eggs, we cut a notch in the tail and throw it back. We don't keep females with eggs. This lets other fishermen know that this is a female with eggs," Lobster John explained as he took a tool and cut a notch in the females tail and threw her back in the water.

"Then we check the size," Lobster John explained as he held up a special gauge to measure the remaining lobster.

"This tool measures the length of the lobster's carapace, or body, from the rear of the eye socket down to the beginning of the tail. The minimum size is 3 ¼ inches and the maximum length is 5 inches. We throw back any lobstah outside that range. These rules are in place to conserve the lobstah population. We don't want to plunder them like some other states have done. If we let the young and the older lobstahs go and the females with eggs, they will continue to thrive and multiply. This is big business in Maine. Each year, over one hundred million pounds of lobstah are caught here in Maine, which brings in hundreds of millions of dollars," Lobster John explained as he tossed back the lobster because it was longer than 5 inches.

We checked on several other traps and scored several lobsters that were within the range to keep. We learned about the lobster claws and how one is different than the other. The larger claw is called the crusher, while the smaller one is the pincer. Lobster John showed us how he puts plastic guards over the claws so no one gets hurt. He explained that lobsters vary in color, but the shells always turn red when you boil them for dinner.

After a while, Lobster John put fishing operations aside and showed us around the coast. We cruised along close to shore, south of Bar Harbor. He pointed out some mansions nestled into the tree covered shore and explained who they belonged to and a few historical tales about them. He pointed out the tallest cliff and explained that hiking the Great Head Trail will take us to the top. We cruised past Thunder Hole and we could see Sand Beach. We turned around near a small island called Old Soaker, and Lobster John pointed up to Otter Cliffs and explained that it is a popular place for technical rock climbers.

We had our first confirmed seal sighting on the ride back to Bar Harbor. We motored past a light house perched on a small rocky island. Our boat slowed down to idle speed and Lobster John cut the power. The island was speckled with hundreds of sea gulls swooping around and squawking.

Lobster John pointed towards the light house on the tiny island and said, "That's the Egg Rock Light House, the smallest lighthouse on the Maine coast. Look at the rocks along the shore and you can see some harbor seals with brown fur. Over there are a few grey seals."

We snapped a few pictures as Lobster John narrated. After sitting off the shore of Egg Rock for several minutes, Lobster John fired up the motor and navigated his boat further out to sea, close to the shore of a small island. Then he cut the power, handed Sarah a pair of binoculars and said, "This is Petit Manan Island, we're close to the

Schoodic Peninsula. If you look closely you might see the Atlantic puffin. These funny looking birds are either all black or white and black, have a broad beak that's bright red and black, and they have orange legs. Years have been spent bringing that sea bird back to this area and they now thrive here."

Sarah spotted one and we all took turns gazing at these pretty birds through her binoculars. After everyone had a chance to see an Atlantic puffin, Lobster John fired up the motor once again and navigated us safely back to the Bar Harbor pier. That boat excursion was amazing! Being on

the water gave me a better feel for Mount Desert Island and why the sea is a huge part of the Acadia National Park experience. As we stepped off Lobster John's vessel, we all thanked him for an awesome tour. He handed us brochures advertising his friend's whale watching excursion and other boat tours offered on MDI.

"There are several fantastic boat charters and cruises that have their own niche that you might enjoy. It was great spending time with all of you," Lobster John said as we thanked him again and walked along the pier back onto land, just as thunder clouds rolled in.

"It looks like rain, so we should hold off on exploring the carriage roads until the storm passes. We could check out the park visitor center or a museum," Arthur suggested.

"Let's start with the park's Hulls Cove Visitor Center and then visit the Sieur de Monts Nature Center. By then, hopefully the storm will have passed," Captain George said.

"Sounds like a plan," Papa Lewis agreed.

We walked a short distance over to the Island Explorer bus stop on the village green in the center of town, and boarded a bus headed to the Hulls Cove Visitor Center, a recommended first stop when you visit Acadia National Park. You can purchase your park pass there and get expert advice on making the most of your Acadia experience. If we didn't already have family in the area, this would have been our first stop on our adventure. The rain was coming down hard as the bus motored along the Park Loop Road.

The Island Explorer dropped us off near a granite staircase that climbs up to the entrance of the Hulls Cove

Visitor Center. There were 52 steps to climb to the top—we joked that this was a good rainy-day hike. An example of a Bates cairn is perched next to the stairs to educate visitors on this type of trail marker. Inside, dozens of people milled about. Some waited in line to get information from park rangers. Others shopped for souvenirs and books, while some studied maps to plan an adventure. Our very own Hug-a-Bug stood in line to show a park ranger that she had completed all the necessary steps to become a Junior Ranger. The ranger reviewed Hug-a-Bug's Junior Ranger book, then asked Hug-a-Bug to raise her right hand as she took the Junior Ranger oath. The park ranger handed Hug-a-Bug a Junior Ranger badge and signed the official Acadia Junior Ranger certificate on the back of the Junior Ranger booklet. A small group of families had gathered nearby to witness the swearing-in ceremony and they all applauded. Hug-a-Bug cracked a proud smile and she thanked the park ranger as she stepped aside for the next child to prove their readiness to become a Junior Ranger. Then we exited the building. The entire time we were there, I kept a look out for signs of Mic, the time-travel watch thief, but he was nowhere in sight.

We marched back down the 52 steps and caught the Island Explorer to the Sieur de Monts Nature Center. This is the location where we time traveled and met the Wabanaki Indians and Dr. Abbe, founder of the Abbe Museum.

As the bus approached the Nature Center, Captain George filled us in on some history. "This was the original main gathering spot in the park in the early days when George Dorr served as the park superintendent. Back then, he was referred to as the park custodian."

We filed off the bus and into the Nature Center. At the center of the room, there was a circular topographical map of Acadia National Park. We gathered around to have a look. The map gave us some perspective on the various locations in the park and the islands nearby.

The walls were lined with interesting facts about weather and nature. One plaque highlighted the area as a super highway for migrating birds. The plaque went on to say that it is estimated that four to ten million birds pass through the area—wow! Some of the birds that are common to the region are the common eider, the Arctic tern, the piping plover, the laughing gull, and the Atlantic puffin. The display had a push button to let you sample each bird sound. We all got excited because we just saw a puffin this morning. As we walked further into the Nature Center, we heard the distinct sound of an owl. We learned that a young barred owl had taken up residence nearby and was not going to wait until nightfall to hoot, like his wise elders.

Environmental scientist reports blanketed the walls with facts and concerns about the warming climate and how it could impact the future of Acadia National Park.

One plaque explored the concerns about the forest. The area has two types of forest, boreal and eastern decid-uous. Boreal is the spruce-fir forest; it consists of balsam fir and red spruce. The deciduous forest are common trees you find elsewhere, such as birch, aspen, oak, maple, and beech. The concern highlighted is that the warming climate could result in less spruce and fir trees. Since we had arrived on MDI, most of the trees we'd noticed had been the spruce-fir trees. As we looked out from Gorham Mountain, that's what sprinkled most of our view. What would take their place? Other concerns centered on the possibility that the sparse foliage on the harsh mountain summits could disappear or change as the climate warms and what would happen to the animal species that thrive on these small and fragile plants.

The Nature Center was loaded with eye opening information on how dramatic an effect warmer weather might have on this area, but what I learned next really caught my attention. Scientists are concerned that the warmer climate may drive the lobster, shrimp, and other marine species that thrive in cold water further north, and other warm water sea life may become the new inhabitants. Scientists have already tracked longfin squid, a species that historically has not thrived north of Massachusetts, in the Gulf of Maine, leading them to believe it is already happening. The Nature Center had an example of what a restaurant menu might look like in 2050. Hint: lobster wasn't on the menu. What would Maine do if the lobsters migrated north? That caught my attention. I live for food. For the last two nights, I had two amazing lobster meals and we just learned from Lobster John all about the lobster industry and how millions of lobsters are caught in the Gulf of Maine annually.

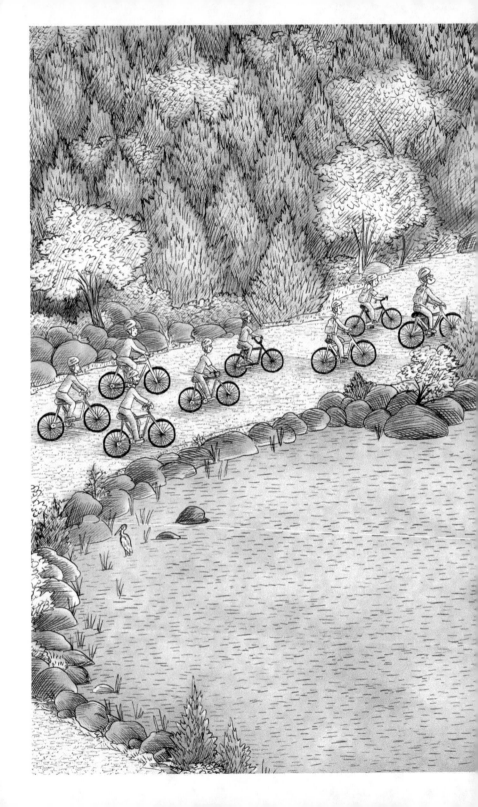

CHAPTER 14

BIKES, CARRIAGES, AND BRIDGES

We stepped out of the Nature Center and noticed that the rain had stopped. The dark clouds had been replaced with blue sky, like a stage set and ready for a new scene.

"They say if you don't like the weather on MDI, wait an hour," Captain George said.

We walked around to the back side of the building, and I noticed a historic marker with an old picture positioned on a post, titled "Acadia's Founding Father." Arthur, Sarah, Hug-a-Bug, and I circled around the picture in hopes of discovering a new clue. There was a picture of this location taken in 1909. Well-dressed people sat in chairs listening to an outdoor concert, and the monument that George Dorr had built over the Sieur de Monts spring was visible in the back ground. The description on the marker told of George Dorr's background in more detail.

"I'll bet many of the people in this picture were the same rich and famous folks that belonged to the Bar Harbor Club where you saw Mic yesterday," Arthur suggested.

"That's it! Why didn't I think of that before? Mic is following the money—that's why he was at the Bar Harbor Club. That's why the few times we saw him in the past, he was visiting places and time periods where the rich people, also known as 'rusticators,' spent time. That also explains why he visited Mr. Dorr's farm, as Mr. Dorr was born into a rich family," I said.

"What do you think he plans to do with our time-travel magic, if his goal is money? Do you have a plan on how to get the watch back?" Sarah asked.

"I'm not sure yet, but I want to test this theory out. Since we don't know the exact date this photo was taken, it would be a waste of time picking a random date to time travel if we want to run into Mic. If we can find a date in this location that we know for sure an event occurred that attracted rich people, we might run into him," I said.

Our parents, grandparents, Captain George, and Fran had circled around us and heard our discussion.

"Bubba Jones, take us back to August 14, 1928,

because on that date, Mr. Dorr held a dedication ceremony for Dr. Abbe's museum. It was privately funded by wealthy people and they all would have been here for that event. Dr. Abbe died before his museum was open to the public," Captain George said.

We all walked behind the Nature Center and along the Jessup Trail until we were out of sight from others. We gathered in a circle and I said, "Take us back to the afternoon of August 14, 1928."

The sky went dark, and a gust of wind pushed against me. Then it was light again. The Nature Center had transformed into an information center. People sat in rows of chairs for a ribbon cutting ceremony that was underway. Everyone was dressed up in fancy suits and dresses, including us. Our families split up and began looking around for Mic. Hug-a-Bug spotted him right away. Mic was sitting in the first row as if he was part of the ceremony. He was laughing and talking with a man seated next to him. We regrouped back in the trees and I took us back to the present. The sky went dark and a gust of wind blew. It was light again and we were standing back on the Jesup Path.

"Did you see Mic laughing and conversing with the gentlemen next to him? He's getting to cozy with people in the past. He's violating the cardinal rule of time travel: don't draw attention to yourself or become the center of attention. We need to get that magic back before he says or does something wrong and messes up history," Captain George stated.

"I think we may have a way to get your time-travel watch back, but it's going to take some more time. Captain George, I think you should continue to show us the island for now," I suggested.

"You got it Bubba Jones. Your family has proven its ability to solve national park mysteries, so whatever you think. Now that the weather has cleared, let's go explore the carriage roads. I just called Commodore Don and he's coming to meet us with his shop van loaded with bikes and helmets," Captain George said.

We walked over to the parking lot where Commodore Don was waiting for us behind the steering wheel of a bus. He had enough bikes for all of us attached to a trailer. We boarded his bus, took a seat, and we were off on another adventure.

As Commodore Don drove, he regaled us with park history. "There are 45 miles of carriage roads in the park and cars are not allowed on them. John D. Rockefeller Jr., the son of wealthy oil man John D. Rockefeller who owned property here, paid for these carriage roads and he was very hands-on with the construction of them. He enjoyed horseback riding and he wanted to create a place to escape into nature without interacting with automobiles. He began construction in 1917 and the roads were completed by 1940. These carriage roads have seventeen unique stone bridges that were specially designed to blend into nature and avoid contact with the island's paved roads and the Park Loop Road. Construction on the Park Loop Road began in 1922 and was completed in the 1950s."

Captain George said, "Grandma Jones, Fran, and Petunia are going to have popovers and tea at the Jordan Pond House while the rest of you ride. Then, I'm going to pick you up and all of us are going to go for a carriage ride—John D. Rockefeller Jr. style."

We pulled off the Park Loop Road and parked in a gravel lot next to a carriage road. Commodore Don hopped out of the bus and we all helped him remove the bikes. Arthur and Sarah handed everyone a helmet and checked to be sure everyone had enough water to drink for the bike ride. Commodore Don hopped back in the bus with Grandma Jones, Fran, and Petunia, waved goodbye, and drove away.

Captain George and Papa Lewis reviewed a map, talked among themselves, and then called us over to share the plan.

"We'll ride the Bubble Pond Loop first and see how everyone feels. Then, if you're all up for it, we'll ride the Eagle Lake Loop carriage roads, too. Sound like a plan?" Captain George asked.

Everyone nodded in agreement as we clipped our helmets on, shouldered our daypacks, saddled onto our bikes, and took off. Arthur and Sarah led us as we peddled under a stone bridge beneath a road and continued along a hard-packed gravel surface about the width of a car. The intersections were marked with wooden signposts designated with a number on the post to make it easy to find your way. Signs hung beneath a wooden arrow to direct us along the right path. The carriage road led us along the edge of Bubble Pond, where the water was calm and still. The road was relatively flat, which made it easy to peddle. Other than a few other cyclists, we were very remote from cars and the hustle and bustle of other tourists. Jagged blocks of rock were placed along the inner edge of the carriage road on the pond side.

"Us locals call those rocks Rockefeller's teeth, but they are really called granite coping stones," Sarah shouted back to us as we peddled along.

While we were on the Bubble Pond Loop, we stopped at one of Rockefeller's bridges where it crossed over a stream. We decided to take a water break and get a closer look at the craftsmanship of the bridge. The bridge was built by hand and made of large granite stone blocks. It looked like something that would lead you up to a castle. We climbed down to the creek beneath the bridge and explored around. Some of the stones had drill marks, which indicated that they had been cut and shaped by man. *Wow! It must have been a huge undertaking to build this bridge and there are sixteen others,* I thought!

We finished the Bubble Pond Loop in a short amount of time and regrouped for a water break and to check to see if everyone was motivated to continue and ride around Eagle Lake. Arthur warned us that the Eagle Lake Loop is a much longer and would take more time to complete. Everyone was fine with that and we all agreed to keep going. The Eagle Lake Loop followed the perimeter of the big lake, like the Bubble Pond Loop. But it was more than two times the distance. When we finished the ride, everyone was sapped of energy. Commodore Don's bus was parked and ready to pick us up when we finished.

"That was amazing! Rockefeller rocks!" I said.

"I agree with Bubba! Two thumbs up!" Hug-a-Bug said.

We helped load the bikes onto the trailer and climbed into the bus. Grandma Jones, Fran, and Petunia were already on board, ready for our carriage ride. Grandma was still smiling with delight from her second popover snack of our trip.

Commodore Don drove us to the Wildwood Stables, where the stable crew were expecting us and had a carriage with enough seats for all of us. We climbed aboard the carriage and sat behind the driver, who sat ready to go with his hands firmly on the horse reins.

When everybody on board was settled, the driver signaled the horses and we were off. We circled Day Mountain and learned that it was once part of the Rockefeller estate. The driver was very knowledgeable and pointed out various geological features and plants, and shared some more interesting Rockefeller history. We made a special stop near the Jordan Pond gatehouse, and stepped off the carriage to look around. Our driver explained that the gatehouse was made of granite stone and bricks and had a high-pitched roof. Rockefeller had two of these built by a prominent architect. An attendant once lived in the gatehouse, and his main job was to keep automobiles off of the carriage roads.

This was our opportunity to time travel back to

meet Rockefeller and to look for Mic. Captain George began to ask the carriage driver questions about how the builders cut the stone to build the gatehouse; this created a diversion (to distract the driver) so that Papa Lewis, Hug-a-Bug, and I could slip around the corner of the gatehouse and travel back in time. When we got around the corner, Papa Lewis suggested that we go back to the first day of summer, 1932. That was the year the gate house was completed.

"Take us back to the first day of summer, 1932," I whispered, holding onto my magic journal.

The sky went dark, a gust of wind blew, then it was light again. Papa Lewis and I wore suits and Hug-a-Bug wore a dress and a sun hat. We walked around the corner and sure enough, there was John D. Rockefeller Jr. standing with George Dorr and Grosvenor Atterbury, the architect of the gatehouse.

"This is more than I ever envisioned. It's a remarkable building and it's much more than a gate to keep automobiles out. Grosvenor, we're going to have you design a few more buildings," John D. Rockefeller Jr. said.

"I agree. The French architecture is impressive and compliments the French history of the area," George Dorr said.

Just then, a man on a horse trotted up and stopped—it was Mic.

The gatekeeper said to Mic, "You may proceed."

Mic dismounted his horse and stood nearby holding the reins instead of riding through the gate. Before we drew attention to ourselves, we walked back around the corner of the gatehouse and time traveled back to the present. We emerged from the side of the gatehouse and Captain George was still in a conversation with the driver about the construction when we all climbed back into the carriage. Their conversation stopped and our driver continued along the carriage road and we soon returned to the Wildwood Stables. Everyone had a great time. It felt good to rest after our bike ride.

CHAPTER 15

SETTLERS AND SECRETS

We thanked the driver for a fun carriage ride and climbed back into Commodore Don's bus. Captain George politely directed Commodore Don to take us to the Carroll Homestead.

"I want to show you how early settlers carved out a living here. The Carroll homestead is a well-preserved example of how families once lived here before Acadia National Park. Sarah and Arthur both took school field trips to the Carroll homestead. I volunteered to come along with their classes. I brushed up on all the facts from the Carroll Homestead Educators Guide, which the National Park has posted on its website," Captain George explained.

On the drive, I explained to everyone what happened when we time traveled at the gatehouse and saw Mr. Rockefeller, Mr. Dorr, Grosvenor Atterbury, and Mic.

"We need to get that watch back from Mic. Bubba Jones, you said you might have an idea. What is it?" Arthur asked.

"I'm not ready to share my idea yet—I need a little more information first. Give me some more time to explore Acadia and MDI," I said.

Our bus pulled up to a small rectangular one-and-a-half-story house. It had weathered gray wood siding and two brick chimneys perched on the roof.

"This is the Mountain House Carroll Homestead. According to the Educator's Guide, John Carroll left Ireland in 1814. He lived for six years in Newfoundland. But in 1820, he set sail for Washington D.C. to find work. He was a mason by trade and heard Washington was hiring skilled masons, but he stopped at MDI along the way. While on the island, he hurt his foot and the daughter of a local family nursed him back to health. He married her and moved into this home. John never made it to D.C.; instead, he carved out a living as a mason on MDI. It looks like we're all alone here. Bubba Jones take us back to June 1831."

"Take us back to June 1831," I said as everyone gathered around me and I put my hand on the magic journal.

The sky went dark, a gust of wind blew, then it was

light again. The bus was gone. Now all the females in our group wore dresses and all of the males wore wool pants with suspenders, white cotton shirts, and leather boots. I could hear a chicken clucking, pigs grunting, and then a cow mooed. A little girl waved as she trekked by with an armload of firewood. Another girl sat on the porch plunging a wood handle into churning butter. Two other girls scrubbed clothes on a washboard and then hung them on a clothes line to dry.

"John and Rachel had six children. All eight of them lived in this small home. They all had to help out around the house," Captain George said.

A woman, holding a small boy in her arms, stood up from picking vegetables in the garden and walked towards us.

"Hi folks, I'm Rachel Carroll. Can I help you?" She said.

"Hi Rachel, we're the Jones family visiting our kin in Bar Harbor. We're looking for a young man named Mic. Have you run across him?" Papa Lewis asked.

"No, I have not. My husband, John, is on the other side of the island building a chimney. He might know more. Can I offer you a slice of blueberry pie?" Rachel Carroll asked.

"That sounds great, but we need to keep our search going. Thank you," Papa Lewis answered.

"Good luck!" Rachel Carroll replied, and she stepped back into the garden and went back to work picking vegetables while holding on to her young son.

We walked into the tree line, away from everyone and out of sight, formed into a tight circle, and I said, "Take us back to the present."

The sky went dark, wind blew me back, and then it was light again. We were back in our modern clothes, standing next to Commodore Don's bus. We all climbed back on board and Commodore Don drove us back towards Bar Harbor.

"Why did you turn down the blueberry pie? That sounded awesome," Hug-a-Bug asked.

"That poor woman would've had to leave her work in the garden to assemble plates and pie for all of us. Then they would have to clean up after us, not to mention that the pie was probably for their dessert," Papa Lewis replied.

"Wow, I never thought about all that. I guess we have it pretty good. We can simply buy a pie from the bakery and put our dirty plates in the dishwasher or use disposables," Hug-a-Bug responded.

"I know it's been a long day for you, but you need to learn some more MDI history and how it involves Captain George and me," Commodore Don said.

"What do you mean?" I asked.

"We're going to take a roundabout way back to Bar Harbor so we can show you a piece of history that might be a motivation for someone to steal our time travel. This piece of history has the both of us really concerned," Captain George added.

Commodore Don passed the turnoff to Bar Harbor and instead, we continued onto the one-way portion of the Park Loop Road, passed Sand Beach, and then Thunder Hole. Commodore Don passed a sign that read "Otter Cliffs," and turned the bus off of the road onto the berm and parked. Commodore Don looked over at Captain George and then began to tell us the story.

"The U.S. Navy operated an important radio relay station here at Otter Cliffs. During World War I, the Navy station at Otter Cliffs helped locate enemy German submarines. In the 1930s, John D. Rockefeller Jr. wanted to build the Park Loop Road along the Otter Cliffs coast, but the Navy base stood in the way. The location of the base on MDI was very strategic for radio signals, so Mr. Rockefeller struck a deal with the Navy to relocate the base to Schoodic Point, in Winter Harbor, another area of Acadia National Park. Mr. Rockefeller went a step further and agreed to help build some of the buildings at the new military complex in the same theme as the carriage road gatehouses.

"The Navy relocated to Schoodic Point in 1935 and remained until it closed in 2001. Captain George and I served in the Navy at this base until it closed—our mission was top-secret. After the base closed, it was handed back over to the National Park Service. Nothing top secret remains; just old buildings. As far as the Navy is concerned, their secrets were removed and have not been compromised. I'm pretty sure the Navy doesn't have a security protocol for a time traveler in search of top secret information, that's our concern," Commodore Don explained.

"What sort of secrets are you talking about? What did you do in the Navy?" I asked.

"We can't give you specifics, but we were both cryptologists. We tracked and located foreign warships to target them and decode their communications. Our mission was to protect the U.S. Navy fleet. Our mission remains top secret," Commodore Don explained.

"Wow! That does give Mic a motive, but what would he gain from stealing old military secrets?" Papa Lewis said.

"The information we have so far on Mic doesn't point to stealing military secrets, but I had no idea this base existed. We should consider this before I share my other theory," I said.

"So, let me get this straight: you and Commodore Don are Navy spies?" Hug-a-Bug asked Captain George.

"What we did is no different then what we're doing right now to protect our family time-travel secret. In fact, the secret codes we sent you were created by our very own family cryptologist," Captain George said.

"Are you our secret family time-travel cryptologist?" Hug-a-Bug asked.

Captain George didn't say anything. He just smiled, which we took as a yes.

"We'll show you the old base so you have a better understanding of what we're talking about. Commodore Don and I put the old Navy base under surveillance as soon as the family time-travel pocket watch was stolen. We went ahead and set up a group camp at Schoodic Woods Campground for everyone tonight so we can show

you the compound and get your opinion. This is a brand
new Acadia National Park campground. We can't exactly
go to the Navy about the time travel concern, because
they would think we are out of our minds. Is everyone
in?" Captain George asked.

Everyone agreed, so Commodore Don started the bus
back up and drove into Bar Harbor. We stopped at our
cousin's home to grab some of our gear for the night and
we also picked up Cadillac. We had to leave him home all
day because we couldn't get him into the visitor centers.
As we all climbed back in the bus, Cadillac did circles
around us in excitement.

Commodore Don drove us down to the pier in Bar
Harbor. We purchased tickets for the Schoodic Ferry cruise,
walked out onto the pier, and boarded the boat. It was a
small vessel and could only hold about twenty-five people.
It had an upper deck above the enclosed pilot house. We
all headed to the upper deck and we were off.

We motored across Frenchman Bay and past the
Porcupine Islands. Captain George pointed out a private
island with a home on it. Imagine living on your own
Island in the Atlantic Ocean. Captain George handed
me a pair of binoculars and directed me to look where
he pointed to see a harbor porpoise, which I saw just as
it jumped out of the water. It resembled a dolphin, but
is classified as a whale. Captain George explained that
they eat 10% of their body weight in fish each day. I
passed the binoculars to Hug-a-Bug to have a look. We
also spotted seals swimming nearby. They looked like tire

innertubes floating in the water. We passed a lighthouse as our boat puttered by Turtle Island, and then we steered into port at Winter Harbor. An Island Explorer bus sat near the dock, ready to pick us up as we exited the boat. We piled on the Island Explorer, which delivered us to the entrance of Schoodic Woods Campground, then Commodore Don led us over to our campsite.

"This is a brand new campground that Acadia National Park just built," Commodore Don explained.

Unlike the older, mature, spruce forest at the Blackwood Campground we stayed in earlier, newly planted bushes and trees sprinkled the landscape. The campground buildings were brand new. Commodore Don led us to two campsites, side by side, each with a large tent all set up and ready to move in. Commodore Don had some of his friends set up camp for us, knowing we would arrive late in the day. The kids took one tent and the adults took the other. Cots and sleeping bags were already inside.

"Now this is luxury camping," I thought.

Commodore Don and Captain George cooked everyone scallops and shrimp pasta using iron pots over an open fire. Then Papa Lewis and Dad broke out s'mores for desert.

"We'll take you to the old Navy base in the morning and show you around Schoodic Point," Captain George said.

We sat around the campfire and relaxed for a little while. There wasn't a lot of conversation; everyone was exhausted from an action-packed day. I went into a trance as I stared into the embers of the fire. We had only been here a few days, but we've been on such a fast-paced adventure, it seemed like a month had gone by. We all helped extinguish the fire and everyone headed off to bed.

The next morning, the aroma of fresh coffee and frying bacon drifted through the tent and woke me up. I quietly unzipped from my sleeping bag, got dressed, and emerged from the tent. It was chilly from the wind blowing in off the ocean. Grandma, Fran, and Mom were cooking eggs and bacon on a propane stove perched on the end of the picnic table, while Papa Lewis brewed coffee in a pot over a separate one-burner hiking stove.

Soon, everyone was up and seated around the picnic table for breakfast. Sea gulls squawked as they flew overhead, reminding us of how close we were to the shore. It was nice to camp with the whole crew. After breakfast, we packed up our gear. Commodore Don explained that his friends would take care of taking the tents down—now that's service.

"I picked up lunch sandwiches and bottles of water for everyone at my friend's deli in Winter Harbor. They're in the cooler for everyone to pack in your day packs," Captain George explained.

"Thanks, Captain George," I said.

Everyone thanked Captain George and Commodore Don for hosting us and we all stuffed a deli sandwich and a bottle of water in our packs. We walked down by the road and in minutes an Island Explorer bus picked us up and we were off toward the old Navy base. The

Island Explorer turned into a drive next to a sign that read: "Schoodic Education and Research Center." The bus screeched to a stop in front of a large, two-story building with a high-pitched roof. It had the similar brick, stone, and wood architecture features as the park gatehouse buildings on MDI.

"This building is Rockefeller Hall and was built for the Navy by Mr. Rockefeller. The Navy and Acadia National Park had a great working relationship, and when the base closed, the park took back ownership. The building was recently renovated and now serves as a research center for the National Park. This was much nicer than your typical Navy barracks," Captain George explained.

We walked a short distance along a path, then we noticed a white van with a telephone company sign on the side, parked in the middle of nowhere. It was backed into the woods, hidden from sight along the trail, and it was surrounded by orange cones that you see near road work.

"Hmmm, that's strange. Why is a telephone company van out here in the bushes?" Hug-a-Bug asked.

"That van belongs to a friend who uses the vehicle as cover so he doesn't cause suspicion. He does not know about our time travel, so don't mention it. I hired him to set up surveillance and report to me if he sees anyone, especially a man, near where the two main secret Navy buildings were once located. I have not heard from him at all. So, we'll get the report from him right now," Captain George explained in a whisper.

Just then, the side door of the van slid open. A grey-haired man similar in age to Captain George stepped out of the side door. Inside the van, a chair faced rows of TV monitors mounted inside behind the driver's seat with multiple video images of the area displaying.

"Hello, Captain George. What did you do, bring the Coast Guard with you? I'm happy to report that I've been very lonely here. Other than an occasional hiker and park staff coming and going from the Schoodic Education Research Center, no one fitting your description has been in the area. I have cameras and motion sensors placed everywhere. What's this all about anyway?" the man asked.

"I'm being overly cautious. I had reason to believe that a man might try and harm the old Navy base. It wasn't enough information to go to the authorities, so I thought your surveillance would be best. Thank you for doing all this. You can call it mission complete and wrap things up," Captain George told his friend.

"Anytime, Captain George, always glad to help. There's nothing left to harm at the base anyway. I'll have my equipment out of here in minutes," the man said.

We waved goodbye and walked back to Rockefeller Hall.

"There's not much left of the old base to see, just old buildings; and it's surrounded by a security fence. The antennae that we used for spying on foreign warships were removed years ago. Well, Bubba Jones, I'm relieved to say, I don't think Mic is after our military secrets.

Thank goodness. My friend is the best in the business. I worked with him in the Navy, and if there was anyone lurking around, he would have found them. Let's head out to see Schoodic Point and explore your idea on how to get that time-travel pocket watch back."

CHAPTER 16

THE PLAN UNFOLDS

We walked a short distance along the road to Schoodic Point. There, massive rocks sprawled along the seashore and a constant pattern of waves crashed against the shore line. It was a natural sea landscape of a rocky seashore and ocean as far as the eye could see, uninterrupted by anything manmade. We all sat out on the rocks and enjoyed the rhythmic calming sound of the surf and the peaceful view for several minutes. Captain George warned us not to get too close to the water because waves often slam the shore unannounced and can pull you in. He pointed over to Little

Moose Island and explained that you can walk out to the island at low tide.

"Bubba Jones, you said you have a theory. Have you come up with a way to get that time-travel watch back? The military motive is off the table, but Mic could alter history with those skills," Captain George said.

Just then the Island Explorer pulled into the parking lot.

"We need to catch that bus to make it to the afternoon ferry back to Bar Harbor. We'll pick this conversation back up on the top deck of the boat," Captain George said.

We all waived for the bus driver to hold on to allow us time to walk up from the shore. In minutes, we arrived at the Winter Harbor dock where the ferry boat was tied up and bobbing in the choppy water.

We boarded the boat and headed back to Bar Harbor. All of us filed up the ladder to the top deck. Other passengers remained below, out of earshot amid the boat engine noise and the wind. Everyone looked at me. They wanted to hear my plan.

"I think Mic is following around rich people from the past and I think he is trying to figure out a way to steal their money. I could be wrong, but whenever we've time traveled, we've only encountered Mic when there were rich and famous people around, like George Dorr and Mr. Rockefeller or the rusticators eating popovers and staying at the Green Mountain House. When we time traveled to historical times without rich people, like meeting the Wabanaki natives or visiting the Carroll Homestead, Mic was not there. My theory really took hold when we encountered Mic at the Bar Harbor Club, a place known for its very rich members in days gone by. You can tell a lot about a person by the books they read. Mic had a book with the name Henry Every in the title. Arthur did an internet search and discovered that Henry Every was a pirate who struck it rich by taking millions of dollars, and then he disappeared back into civilian life. I think he is trying to figure out a way that he can pirate the wealth from millionaires and then disappear. I haven't figured out the connection to the other book, *Bar Harbor: A Town Almost Lost,*" I explained.

"I know that book! It's a pictorial of the historic mansions in Bar Harbor before and after the devastating fire of 1947. The Bar Harbor Historical Society has a nice little museum with photos and memorabilia about the fire, but of course we can always time travel and witness it first hand," Captain George said.

"I'm not sure why Mic would be so interested in the fire. We should check it out though when we get to Bar Harbor. I have an idea on how we can get that time-travel pocket watch back. It will require everyone's help and the help of others as well," I said.

"What do you have in mind, Bubba Jones?" Papa Lewis asked.

"We need to set a trap for Mic and I have an idea about how to do it. First, we need someone to reserve a reception room at the Bar Harbor Club. We will host a special event called 'Meet the Rich and Famous People That Once Vacationed Here.' We will advertise the event all over town and invite everyone. Most people will think it's a history program. But Mic will see this as an opportunity to learn more about how he can steal the wealth of people from the past using our time-travel magic. We will set up a security check point at the entrance, just like they do at ball games, amusement parks, and airports, with real security staff. Our reason will be that we have some rich and famous guests and we must assure them that they will be safe. Everyone will have to empty their pockets and place them in a bowl and then walk separately through a metal detector. When Mic goes through the security checkpoint, that will be our opportunity to get the time-travel watch back. We will switch the time-travel watch with a replica look alike. This will take a lot of planning and work. What do you think?" I asked.

"Wow, this could work! Fran has connections with the owner of the Bar Harbor club. Booking the room is right up her alley. My friend that did surveillance at my old Navy base has all the equipment and staff to set up a security check point. We know a jeweler friend in town that might be able to help us create a watch replica. Commodore Don advertises his business all the time. He might be able to help us with publicity. Let's make this happen. Let's get that watch back!" Captain George said.

Papa Lewis gathered everyone in a circle and instructed us to put one hand on top of each other's in the center of the circle. When everyone had a hand stacked on top of someone else's, he said, "Our mission is to use our time travel to protect our natural wildlands. When we are challenged, we must stick together. This is one of those times. We share a special secret, handed down to us for a special reason, to protect our wildlands. Our mission existed before the creation of the National Park Service. Today, our family continues to carry out its mission in conjunction with the National Park Service. Our time-travel ability was not meant to alter history or to harm others. Our current mission is to work together to get that time-travel watch back," Papa Lewis said.

All of us lifted our hands together and then pulled away in a silent family handshake. Papa Lewis gave us the pep talk we needed. Everyone was reminded of our heritage and how important our family mission was—it was an inspirational moment. I had lost track of time until the boat captain announced on the loud speaker that we were approaching Bar Harbor. For the other passengers, that meant departing the boat for another tour destination. For us, that meant we would execute our plan to get that watch back.

As soon as the ferry boat was tied up to the Bar Harbor pier, we filed off and followed cousin Arthur down West Street, and then onto Eden Street.

"If Mic is after money, he might be looking for a way to do it during all the commotion of the 1947 fire. According to the National Park website this fire burned over seventeen thousand acres, including thousands of acres of Acadia National Park. What Mic might be after are the valuables stashed away in Millionaire's Row, which used to run down this street along Frenchman Bay. The fire wiped out 68 enormous mansions, as well as many local resident's homes. These mansions were summer cottages of the rich and famous and none of them were ever rebuilt. We learned about the '47 fire in history class at school. The fire first started in a garbage dump on October 17th during a very dry season. It had not rained all summer or fall. On the afternoon of October 23rd, Millionaire's Row burned to the ground. The fire burned until November 14th; almost a whole month. The business district survived, but many of the mansions did not," Arthur explained.

"I don't think Mic is going to strike it rich from the owners of the mansions. They would have already left town for the winter when the fire broke out," Papa Lewis stated.

"Let's check it out," I said.

We all slipped out of view behind a stand of trees and gathered together.

"Take us back to the morning of October 23, 1947," I said.

Everything went dark, then a gust of wind whipped me around. All of the sudden it was light again and we now stood in front of a huge mansion. Across the lawn stood another mansion and beyond that, another. They just kept going all the way up the street, along the ocean toward this huge plume of smoke and fire that seemed to be moving fast in our direction. It smelled like burning wood, and even though we were over a mile from the fire, I could feel the heat.

An old-fashioned fire truck drove down the street and stopped alongside a moving truck. The driver of the truck stepped out to talk to the firemen—it was Mic! I walked closer to listen to the conversation without Mic noticing me. Mic told the firemen that he was there to help anyone that wanted to secure their valuables from the fire, but the firemen told him that the owners of these estates are already gone for the season—just like Papa Lewis had said. I ran back to our group and told them what I heard. We slipped behind some bushes out of sight and I said, "Take us back to the present."

The sky went dark, wind whipped me around, then it was light again. The mansions were gone and replaced with modern hotels and smaller, averaged sized homes.

"We don't have much time to get that watch back! Mic might not have had any luck with his 1947 plot, but we don't know what he'll think up next," I said.

"That fire must have been horrible. What about all the forest animals and the trees?" Hug-a-Bug said with concern in her voice.

"Fire is a natural occurrence in forests. Most of the spruce and fir forest was replaced with deciduous forest. Animals instinctively dig in, jump in the water, or run away from fire. From what we learned in school, there were only a few human deaths from the fire," Arthur said.

CHAPTER 17

TRAILS, RAILS, AND SWIMMING HOLES

The week flew by as we got ready for our event to get the watch back from Mic. In between preparing for our mission, a family friend of Captain George and Fran, known simply as Trailhead, took us all on some grand MDI adventures. Trailhead grew up with Fran and Captain George, but he is not a time traveler, so Hug-a-Bug and I were instructed to not talk about anything time travel with him. We quickly discovered that there was no time to discuss time travel. Trailhead had us on a new adventure every waking moment in between preparing for our mission.

Trailhead runs a local guide service and leads people all around the island and in Acadia National Park. He took us on a hike up the fabled Beehive. This was a difficult trail and anyone afraid of heights should sit this one out. No dogs were allowed either, so Cadillac had to stay back. Grandma and Captain George sat this one out, too. The trail climbed along a cliff edge, from the Sand Beach area, up rock steps set in place a century ago. We clung onto iron rungs pounded into the side of the mountain, up iron ladders, and over a short iron rung cliff edge bridge. As we inched up the mountain and above the trees we could see a stunning panoramic view of Sand Beach and the ocean. This was a challenging hike.

We hiked down the backside of the Beehive to a pond known as the Bowl, and then hiked back to the Sand Beach parking area to meet up with Grandma Jones and Captain George and Cadillac. All of us hiked the Great Head Trail with more spectacular views of the open ocean sprinkled with sailboats, lobster boats, tour cruises, and excellent views of the rocky seashore.

The next day, we were going to climb the Precipice, the park's most difficult trail with cliff edge climbing like the Beehive. Trailhead described it as a climb up iron rungs and ladders along a massive rock face. Trailhead said that we proved ourselves on the Beehive and would be able to handle the Precipice, but when he checked with the National Park Service website, there was an advisory posted that the Precipice was temporarily closed due to the presence of a peregrine falcon nest. The peregrine is a bird of prey which hunts other birds by swooping down onto them in midair at 200-miles per hour. They were once almost extinct and were on the endangered species list, but they have made a comeback and are no longer an endangered species.

Trailhead took us on another adventure instead, along the Beech Cliff Loop on Beech Mountain. From the top of the mountain we could see out across Echo Lake to the waters of Somes Sound, an inlet off the ocean, and the more distant open ocean. As we descended the mountain, a porcupine walked out from the brush and stood on the trail. It didn't budge and we froze in place and just watched it. The porcupine's grey body was covered with prickly quills.

"Don't walk towards it, those rodents have sharp quills that come off when touched. Slowly back away to give it some space," Trailhead cautioned.

We all followed his advice and backed away slowly. After a few minutes, it wobbled off the trail and into the forest. We capped off the hike with a swim at Echo Lake, near where we had parked our Jeep for the hike. Echo Lake, like other lakes on the island, was carved out by glaciers during the ice age. It had a sandy beach and the water was much warmer than the ocean.

The next day, Commodore Don took us out for another kayaking adventure. This time, we paddled out of Northeast Harbor and followed along the shoreline of Bear Island, a small island just off the coast. We took several pictures of the Bear Island Lighthouse perched high above us on a rocky cliff. This was a good workout, and when we returned to the harbor, I was exhausted, but I now felt confident in my kayaking skills.

After our kayak adventure, we ate our packed lunch and then caught an afternoon boat cruise on the Sea Princess out of Northeast Harbor, narrated by a retired Acadia National Park ranger and naturalist. We motored into Somes Sound, a narrow inlet leading from the ocean in between a rocky cliff shoreline. We learned that Somes Sound used to be classified as a fjord but the Maine Geological Survey changed the classification to a fjard. To be a fjord, in addition to having a steep sloping shore line, the water must have a dead zone (area with no oxygen). Apparently, the sea water flushes completely through Somes Sound and there is no dead zone.

We cruised by a 40 million-dollar mansion. Our naturalist explained how boats use the lighthouse signals to navigate. We motored past Bear Island and Sutton Island over to Little Cranberry Island, which was settled in the late 1700s. We docked at the island pier and walked over to the Islesford Historical Museum: an old red brick building. It was loaded with pictures and artifacts of more than two centuries of island life and the lobster fishing community. The volunteer working at the museum was a descendent of the man who founded the museum in 1926, William Otis Sawtelle.

On the cruise, back to Northeast Harbor, we stopped

the boat along the shore of Sutton Island to view an osprey nest. The nest looked like something out of the dinosaur age; a massive birds nest the size of a large bucket was perched on top of pyramid shaped rock several feet above the sea and away from shore. A baby osprey's head stuck up out of the nest with its beak open waiting for mama to bring it some food. Ospreys are birds of prey that eat fish. After the Sea Princess delivered us safely back to shore, we exited the boat loaded with tons of cool facts about the area.

Finally, the day of our mission arrived, but the event wouldn't start until 7:00 p.m. We had everything all planned and set, so Mom and Dad treated everyone to a late afternoon whale watching cruise. We boarded a boat much larger than the lobster boat and ferry boats we had been on. It had an enclosed seating area and an open deck. This boat was also much faster than the other boats we'd been on. We headed out to sea, miles from shore.

"The Gulf of Maine is home to several species of whales. The humpback, the finback, the minke, and the right whale. Whales are warm blooded mammals. They give birth and breathe air like humans. Each species varies in size. They can eat lots of fish," the captain narrated over a loud speaker.

All of a sudden, a large whale lurched completely out of the water and splashed back under again. We all jumped back in surprise as we snapped photos.

"That was a humpback whale that just breeched. They like to entertain my cruise guests," the Captain explained.

"What does breech mean?" Hug-a-Bug asked.

Captain George explained that a breech is when a whale jumps completely out of the water.

Another whale blew water out of its blow hole further out in the distance, away from our boat. It then disappeared under water and reappeared near our boat and stuck its head up and seemed to look right at us. That same humpback whale that did a full breech entertained us for a while before we motored back to Bar Harbor.

We regrouped at our cousin's house to review our plan.

Captain George showed us the imitation pocket watch. The town jeweler was able to doctor up an antique pocket watch using an old photo. It had the same engraved quote as the real watch, "Learn from the past to protect the future." It looked so close to the actual watch that Captain George had his initials "CG" carved on the back side so we could tell the real watch from the imitation.

"That looks exactly like our time-travel watch!" Arthur stated excitedly.

Word about our event was all over town. Commodore Don reported that radio ads aired all week. The town newspaper ran an ad every day. Signs were posted in shop windows all along Main Street. Hotels handed out fliers to guests.

Fran said, "The Bar Harbor Club has been receiving calls and emails all week." She went on to say, "We have a nice event planned with dinner and entertainment. We're serving your choice of lobster bake or shrimp pasta. We have a local pianist booked to play during the reception as everyone arrives. For the main event, we have several presentations by local historians and National Park staff that will share slides and stories about the millionaires and famous people that once vacationed here and how they helped. We advertised the event as a fundraiser and ticket sale proceeds will benefit the Friends of Acadia, a non-profit group that supports the park."

"We even trained Cadillac for a role in our mission," Sarah added with a smile.

"We rented a limousine and hired an elderly man

and woman to dress up in formal clothes and ride in the back," Captain George explained. "They will pull up under the canopy of the entrance accompanied by two men dressed as secret service agents, complete with coiled wire ear pieces and dark suits. Just inside the front door, my friend will have a security check point with a metal detector and a separate table with baskets to place your valuables in when you step through the metal detector."

We each reviewed our roles, dressed up in suits and dresses and then we walked up to the Bar Harbor Club in two separate groups. Arthur and Sarah sat just inside the entrance way, but out of view of people entering the building, so Mic wouldn't be scared away if he saw them. Cadillac wore a yellow fluorescent vest that said "Security K-9" and sat between Arthur and Sarah. Mom and Grandma accompanied Fran and Captain George in the reception hall to greet guests. Dad, Commodore Don, Hug-a-Bug, and I sat outside near the entrance—the trap was set.

CHAPTER 18

ACADIA – WELL WORTH THE TRIP

Guests began arriving thirty minutes before the start of the event. At 6:45 p.m., right on schedule, the limousine pulled up. Two men posing as secret service agents stepped out of the limo, opened the backseat car door, and escorted a well-dressed couple from the car into the building. They looked like elected officials, or at least very important people that require security. The timing couldn't have been more perfect. Mic walked up to the entrance of the club just as the couple from the limousine were escorted inside the building. Meanwhile, the limousine sat beneath the canopy with a secret service agent guarding it.

I texted Arthur, "Mic is about to walk in."

"Got it," Arthur texted back.

As soon as Mic stepped into the entrance, we rushed up to the door and slipped inside behind him. If Mic turned around to leave after seeing the security set up, Captain George would command the security staff to apprehend him for suspicious behavior, and Commodore Don and Dad planned to block the door so he couldn't escape. Hopefully, it wouldn't come to that. Thankfully, Mic cooperated and emptied his pockets into the bowl. Surprisingly, there was no pocket watch.

Crud. All this for nothing. He doesn't have the time-travel watch, I thought to myself.

When Mic stepped through the metal detector, the sensor beeped and the security guards asked him to step back in order to double check to make sure he had removed everything from his pockets. Mic pulled the pocket watch out from his suit jacket and unfastened the chain from his shirt button. He cautiously set it in the bowl and kept his eyes glued on it as he separated himself from the watch to walk through the metal detector. Just then, Cadillac came running up to the security table and bit the basket containing the time-travel pocket watch with his teeth. The security guard sitting at the table reached out to grab the basket out of Cadillac's mouth, but the dog was too fast and ran past the guard and around the corner to where Arthur sat. Arthur dropped the fake time-travel watch into the basket, grabbed the real one, and slipped it into his pocket. A second later, the security guard and Mic rounded the corner. The security guard grabbed the basket which was sitting on the floor next to Cadillac.

Whew, that was close! I thought to myself.

"What's that dog doing here? Give me my stuff back," Mic said as he grabbed the basket out of the security guard's hand and quickly slipped the fake time-travel watch into his pocket.

Arthur walked away and into the nearby bathroom where Captain George was waiting for him. Arthur gave Captain George the time-travel watch. Then, Arthur walked back out of the restroom and returned to where Cadillac and Sarah sat. Next, Captain George exited the bathroom, walked out of the front entrance of the club, and handed the real time-travel pocket watch to Commodore Don to hold on to until the event was over.

Mic finished securing all his belongings back in his pockets, then he looked up at Arthur with a suspicious look. He must have recognized Arthur from Mr. Dorr's farm because Mic reached back in his pocket and pulled out the fake time-travel watch. He looked up at Arthur and looked at the watch. He seemed suspicious that something happened, but didn't know exactly what, and then he walked into the reception.

We all sat down at a table together. Mic sat nearby at another table and kept looking over at us. I think it sunk in that something happened, but he still didn't know his watch had been switched. Now that we had safely secured the real time-travel pocket watch, everyone was relieved, and we didn't have to worry about Mic recognizing us anymore. I wondered when he would discover that he could no longer time travel and that his watch is a replica. He must have attempted to time travel during the program because he left the room for a while and when he returned, he approached us with one of the security guards from the front door.

The security guard approached Arthur and tapped him on the shoulder, "Excuse me, this gentleman thinks that you took his watch and replaced it with a different one."

"Why would I do that? Is something wrong with your watch? Did my dog break it? If he did, we will pay to have it repaired," Arthur said looking at Mic.

The security guard held Mic's watch up to his ear, looked at the face of it, and then said, "It works. It's ticking, the hands are moving, and the time is correct."

"But, you don't understand, the real watch was magical. You could time travel with it. Ask him, he'll tell you," Mic pleaded pointing to Arthur.

"Time travel? Wow, that would be so cool, if you could really do such a thing," I chimed in.

"I know you're all time travelers. I was so close to striking it rich until you ruined it and took my time-travel watch," Mic said.

"Okay, that's it, buddy. You're bothering our guests with foolish time-travel nonsense. I'm going to have to ask you to leave," the security guard said to Mic as he was joined by another security guard to be escorted out of the building.

"Sorry to bother you—enjoy the rest of the show," the

security guard said to us as he led Mic away.

Thank goodness no one believed Mic's time-travel story. Even if they searched Arthur, they would not have found the other watch and Mic is the one who stole the time-travel watch in the first place. We simply took back what was ours and possibly saved the world from Mic's "get rich" scheme.

The dinner was a complete success! Our mission was complete. We had safely retrieved the stolen time-travel pocket watch. The pianist and presenters at the event received a standing round of applause at the end of the night. Fran took the stage to announce that, based on ticket proceeds, the Friends of Acadia would receive a check for $16,000. No one ever questioned who the fake famous couple were with the secret service. As it turned out, one of the attendees was an actual descendent of one of the wealthy families that owned a mansion on Millionaire's Row that was lost in the 1947 fire and left an anonymous donation to match all the ticket sales, bringing the grand total of funds raised for the Friends of Acadia to $32,000.

Acadia National Park is a magical place. We were on the island for 14 days, but there was still much more to explore. We didn't have time to do everything. There were some islands we didn't see, more trails left to hike, more museums to gain new facts and knowledge from, more harbors to visit, lighthouses to see, and sunrises to enjoy. It was easy see why the rusticators made this their summer vacation destination, and why so many people have called this place home.

The end of an adventure gives reason for a new one. The next morning, we all gathered for breakfast. Commodore Don joined us and returned the time-travel pocket watch to its rightful owners, Arthur and Sarah. From now on, they would take extra care to make sure no one could ever take their magic watch again. After breakfast, we took down the wall of clues from the map room. Everyone was quiet with sadness that our Acadia Adventure had come to a close. As we loaded up our gear onto the roof rack of the Jeep, I could hear the deep rhythmic thud of drums accompanied by chanting voices.

"The Wabanaki people are having a festival. You can see their ceremonial dances, hear their songs, and buy their baskets in modern time. Do you want to check it out?" Arthur asked us.

Hug-a-Bug and I looked over to our mom and dad for approval.

"That sounds fun, let's go," Dad said approvingly.

We all walked up to the park in the center of town and watched the Wabanaki perform various dances and songs. A group of men sat in a circle each beating a stick on the same drum and chanting tribal songs. Several of the Wabanaki danced and wore traditional tribal dress. Mom bought several of their beautiful hand-made baskets. It was good to see that the tribe is still active in the area.

"You haven't been to Acadia until you try the best ice cream in the world," Sarah said convincingly.

"It's our treat," Captain George chimed in.

"Yeah, it's the least we can do to thank you for all your help to solve our mystery. Without you guys, we might have never got that time-travel watch back," Arthur said in a serious tone.

"I'm glad we could help and let us know if you ever need us again. I would love to come back to explore more of Acadia National Park," I said.

We all walked down the street from the park to an ice cream parlor on Main Street, where a sign touted, "Homemade Ice Cream."

One by one, everybody ordered ice cream cones. I asked for a scoop of Maine blueberry chocolate chip. After everyone had their ice cream cones, we all sat down at a picnic table outside.

While we were eating our ice cream, Fran pulled an envelope out of a bag she carried and said, "Bubba Jones, I checked my mailbox at the hotel this morning and this was addressed to you. I thought that was odd for you to get mail up here."

I was caught by surprise. Who could this be from? I thought as I tore open the letter.

"Dear Bubba Jones and Time-Travel family,

You will find a coded message when you get home. Your help is needed in another National Park right away.

Sincerely,

A Relative"

I licked my ice cream cone and smiled as I looked over at my family, I noticed that they were smiling too, knowing that another adventure was out there waiting for us.

The End.

Hug-a-Bug's Timeline

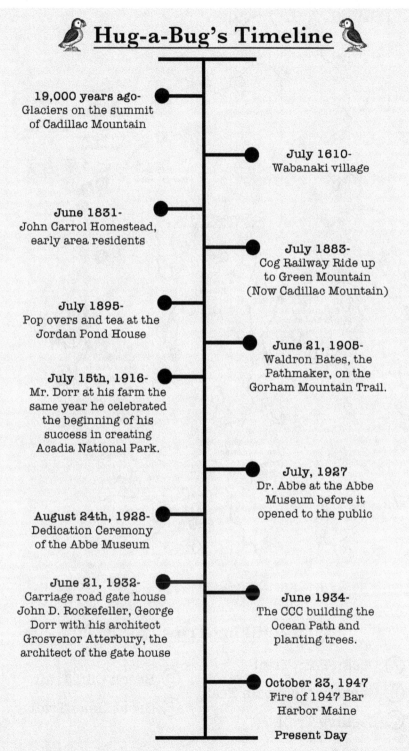

19,000 years ago-
Glaciers on the summit
of Cadillac Mountain

July 1610-
Wabanaki village

June 1831-
John Carrol Homestead,
early area residents

July 1883-
Cog Railway Ride up
to Green Mountain
(Now Cadillac Mountain)

July 1895-
Pop overs and tea at the
Jordan Pond House

June 21, 1905-
Waldron Bates, the
Pathmaker, on the
Gorham Mountain Trail.

July 15th, 1916-
Mr. Dorr at his farm the
same year he celebrated
the beginning of his
success in creating
Acadia National Park.

July, 1927
Dr. Abbe at the Abbe
Museum before it
opened to the public

August 24th, 1928-
Dedication Ceremony
of the Abbe Museum

June 21, 1932-
Carriage road gate house
John D. Rockefeller, George
Dorr with his architect
Grosvenor Atterbury, the
architect of the gate house

June 1934-
The CCC building the
Ocean Path and
planting trees.

October 23, 1947
Fire of 1947 Bar
Harbor Maine

Present Day

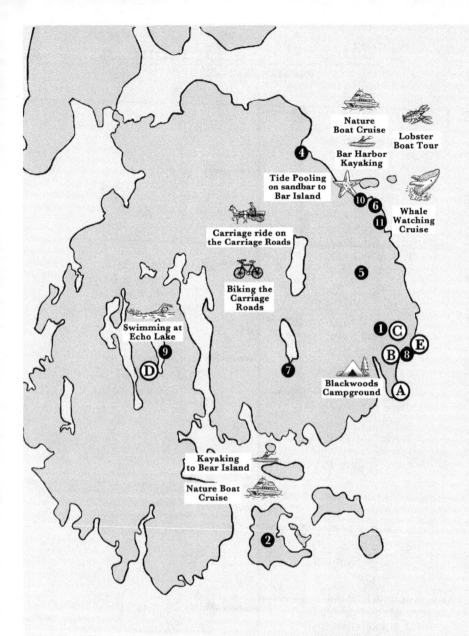

Nature Boat Cruise

Lobster Boat Tour

Bar Harbor Kayaking

Tide Pooling on sandbar to Bar Island

Whale Watching Cruise

Carriage ride on the Carriage Roads

Biking the Carriage Roads

Swimming at Echo Lake

Blackwoods Campground

Kayaking to Bear Island

Nature Boat Cruise

👣 Hiking Trips 👣

Ⓐ Ocean Path Trail

Ⓑ Gorham Mountain Trail

Ⓒ Beehive Trail

Ⓓ Beech Cliff Trail

Ⓔ Great Head Trail

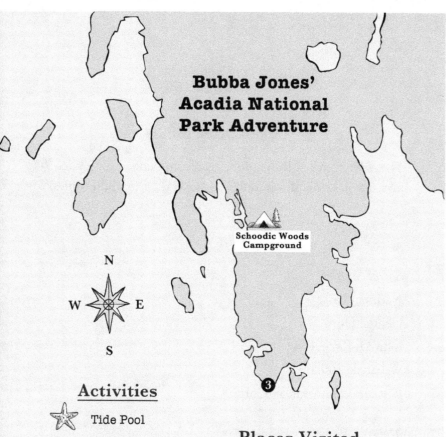

Bubba Jones'
Acadia National
Park Adventure

Schoodic Woods
Campground

N
W • E
S

3

Activities

 Tide Pool

 Campgrounds

 Kayaking

 Swimming

 Nature Cruise

 Biking

 Whale Watching

 Lobster Boat Tour

Carriage Ride

Places Visited

1 Cadillac Mountain

2 Cranberry Island

3 Schoodic Point

4 Hulls Cove Visitor Center

5 Sieur de Mont Nature Center

6 Abbe Museum in the park

7 Jordan Pond House

8 Sand Beach

9 Echo Lake

10 Bar Harbor Club

11 Shore Path, Bar Harbor

CURRICULUM GUIDE

The Adventures of Bubba Jones is recommended for grades 3-7 and may be a helpful resource for several curriculum topics.

Social Studies
National Parks
George Dorr
John D. Rockefeller Jr.
Wabanaki Indians
Civilian Conservation Corps.

Science
Atlantic puffin
Climate change
Geology/ Ancient rocks and mountains
Gulf of Maine
Grey seals
Harbor seals
Intertidal sea life
Lobster
Migratory birds
Seals
Peregrine Falcon
Whales

The Adventures of Bubba Jones
DISCUSSION QUESTIONS

Chapter 1

1. Why are Bubba Jones and his family in Acadia?

2. Why did Captain George pretend he didn't know Papa Lewis in the Cadillac Summit Center?

Chapter 2

1. What is a Glacial Erratic?

2. What kind of railway used to be in Acadia?

3. Can you list two of the rules of time travel?

Chapter 3

1. What is a popover?

2. How many restaurants are in Acadia?

Chapter 4

1. Why did the Jones' family go to another location to see the sunset again?

2. Why did Arthur and Sarah have Bubba Jones take their picture?

Chapter 5

1. What do Arthur and Sarah use to time travel, and what happened to that item?

2. How did the two families plan to communicate?

3. Who was George Dorr?

Chapter 6

1. Why did they go to George Dorr's home?

2. How did they figure out who stole the time-travel watch?

Chapter 7

1. Who are the Wabanaki people?

2. Who was Dr. Abbe?

Chapter 8

1. What is the plan for getting the watch back?

2. What do you think Captain George and Papa Lewis were talking about?

Chapter 9

1.   Who were the CCC?

2.   What is the purpose of the Bates cairn?

Chapter 10

1.   Where do you think the thief went?

2.   What is a tide pool? What kind of creatures live in these habitats?

Chapter 11

1.   What are the two types of seals in Acadia?

2.   What did Papa Lewis and Bubba Jones find out about the thief?

Chapter 12

1.   Why do you think it's important to track where they found Mic?

2.   What is a lobster buoy?

Chapter 13

1.   What are some of the rules to decide which lobsters you can keep?

2.   Can you name some bird species that live in Acadia?

3.   What kind of trees can be found on MDI?

Chapter 14

1. Who was George Dorr?

2. What did John D. Rockefeller Jr. do for the park?

3. How many bridges are on the carriage roads?

Chapter 15

1. Who was John Carrol?

2. What relation did Acadia have with the Navy?

Chapter 16

1. What does Bubba Jones think Mic is after?

2. How does Bubba Jones plan on getting the watch back?

Chapter 17

1. What kinds of whales live in the Gulf of Maine?

2. Is Somes Sound a fjord or a fjard?

Chapter 18

1. What role did Cadillac play in getting the time-travel watch back?

2. What did everyone eat at the end of the book?

3. What was your favorite part of the book and why?

BIBLIOGRAPHY

A Guide to Lobstering in Maine, Maine Department of Marine Resources, July, 2009, assessed, July 2, 2017.

Abrell, Diana, *The Carriage Roads of Acadia National Park, 3rd Edition*, Camden, ME, Down East Books, 2011

Acadia National Park Fact Sheet-Acadia National Park Centennial 2016, Acadia Centennial Task Force, accessed, November 11, 2016, http://www.acadiacentennial2016.org/about-acadias-centennial/media-resources/anp-fact-sheet/

Acadia National Park & Bar Harbor Maine, All Trips - Acadia National Park, accessed June 5, 2017, https://www.acadianationalpark.com/

Acadia National Park Junior Ranger Activity Book

Acadia Visitor, accessed June 6th, 2017, https://www.acadiavisitor.com/

Alt, Jeff. The Adventures of Bubba Jones: Time Traveling Through Shenandoah National Park, New York City, NY, Beaufort Books Publishers, 2016.

Alt, Jeff. The Adventures of Bubba Jones: Time Traveling Through the Great Smoky Mountains, New York City, NY, Beaufort Books Publishers, 2015.

Alt, Jeff. Get Your Kids Hiking: How to Start Them Young and Keep it Fun!, New York City, NY: Beaufort Books Publishers, 2013.

Anderson, Craig J., *Maine fishermen landed a record $616.5 million catch last year*, Press Herald, March 4, 2016, accessed July 2, 2017, http://www.pressherald.com/2016/03/04/maine-fish-seafood-hit-record-616-5-million-in-2015/

Andrews, Evan, Henry Every's Bloody Pirate Raid, History.com, September 4, 2015, accessed July 7, 2017, http://www.history.com/news/henry-everys-bloody-pirate-raid-320-years-ago

Bachelder, Peter D., *Steam to the Summit: The Green Mountain Railway, Bar Harbor's Remarkable Cog Railroad*, Ellsworth, ME, Breakwater Press, 2005

Bar Harbor Club, accessed, December 3, 2017, https://www.barharborclub.com/

BIBLIOGRAPHY

Bar Harbor Inn, accessed, May 27, 2017, https://barharborinn.com/

Clement, Stephanie, Voicemail Correspondence, Conservation Director, Friends of Acadia, March, 2018

Cross, Robert, *The Idle Pleasures of Acadia*, June 23, 1996, Chicago Tribune, accessed, June 13, 2017, http://www.chicagotribune.com/lifestyles/travel/chi-960623onpacadia-story.html

Dorr, George B. *The Story of Acadia National Park*, Bar Harbor ME, Acadia Publishing Company, 1997

Down East Acadia, accessed, June 13, 2017, https://www.downeastacadia.com/

Dyer, Deborah M. *Bar Harbor: A Town Almost Lost: A Pictorial Essay of Bar Harbor's Mansions Before & After the Fire of 1947*, Bar Harbor, ME, Bar Harbor Historical Society, 2008

Exploreacadia.com, accessed March 11, 2017, http://exploreacadia.com/

Epp, Ronald H. *Creating Acadia National Park: The Biography of George Buckman Dorr*, Bar Harbor, ME, Friends of Acadia, 2016

Evans Gollin, Lisa. *An Outdoor Guide to Acadia National Park,* Seattle, WA, The Mountaineers, 1997

Francis, James E. Francis Sr., lecture and Email Correspondence, Director of Cultural & Historic Preservation, The Penobscot Nation, March, 2018

Friends of Acadia Journal, Volume 21, No. 1, Bar Harbor, ME, Friends of Acadia, 2016

Graf, Mike, *Acadia National Park: Eye of the Whale*, Guilford, CT, Falcon Guides, 2013

Graves, Liz, Carrol Homestead Offers Glimpse Back in Time, Mount Desert Islander, July 14, 2016, Accessed, June 6, 2017, https://www.mdislander.com/acadia-centennial-2/carroll-homestead-offers-glimpse-back-time

Hartford, Greg, Acadiamagic.com, Accessed February 12, 2017, http://www.acadiamagic.com/contact.html

Hornsby, Stephen J., Champlain and the Settlement of Acadia, Canadian American Center, Accessed June 8, 2017, https://umaine.edu/canam/publications/st-croix/champlain-and-the-settlement-of-acadia-1604-1607/

Kaiser, James, *Acadia: The Complete Guide, 3rd Edition*, Destination Press & ITS Licensors, 2010

King-Wrenn, Kim and Laurie Hobbes-Olson, The Carroll Homestead: An Educator's Guide to a 19th Century Maine Coastal Homestead, Acadia National Park, Bar Harbor, ME, 1996.

Kish, Carey, *Maine Mountain Guide: AMC's Comprehensive Guide to Hiking Trails of Maine, featuring Baxter State Park and Acadia National Park, 10th Edition*, Boston, MA, Appalachian Mountain Club Books, 2012

Kong, Dolores and Ring, Dan, *Best Easy Day Hikes: Acadia National Park, Second Edition*, Guilford, CT, Falcon Guides, 2011

Maine Lobster, Accessed June 14, 2017, http://maine-lobster.com/lobster-facts

Maine Lobster Facts, Accessed June 14, 2017, https://getmainelobster.com/225/maine-lobster-facts/maine-lobster-facts/

Monkman, Jerry and Marcy. *Discover Acadia National Park: AMC's Guide to the Best Hiking, Biking, and Paddling, 3rd Edition*. Boston, MA, Appalachian Mountain Club Books, 2010

Otter Cliff, Acadia National Park, Accessed June 23, 2017, http://www.barharbormagic.com/acadia/otter-cliff.html

Overton, Penelope, *New Rules Aim to Boost Herring Supply Prized As Lobster Bait*, Press Herald, May 8, 2017, Accessed July 2, 2017, http://www.pressherald.com/2017/05/08/regulators-take-steps-to-protect-herring-fishery/

Playground of the rich & famous. *Portland monthly*, June 2016.

Sarnacki, Aislinn, 11 Things You Might Not Know About Acadia National Park, But Should, Bangor Daily News, Accessed June 5th, 2017, https://bangordailynews.com/2015/04/22/outdoors/11-things-you-might-not-know-about-acadia-national-park-but-should/

Schmitt, Catherine, *Historic Acadia National Park: The Stories Behind One of America's Great Treasures*, Guilford, CT, Rowman & Littlefield, 2016

Skurzynski, Gloria and Alane Fearson, *Out of the Deep: A Mystery in Acadia National Park*, Washington, D.D., National Geographic, 2008

St. Germain, Tom, *A Walk in the Park: Acadia's Hiking Guide*, Bar Harbor, ME, Bar Harbor Enterprises, 2015

Tapley, Lance, Fire Escape, *One Writer's Earliest Childhood memory: Fleeing the Blaze that Forever Changed Bar Harbor*, Down East, Special collector's Edition, June, 2016, Accessed June 24, 2016, https://downeast.com/acadia-fire-escape/

The Navy at Schoodic Point, Schoodicinstitute.org, Accessed, January, 2017, https://www.schoodicinstitute.org/about/navy-schoodic-point/

The Way of the Pirates, Accessed December 16, 2017, http://www.thewayofthepirates.com/famous-pirates/henry-every/

Trotter, Bill, *Acadia officials dedicate renovated Rockefeller building at Schoodic Point*, Bangor Daily News, July 3, 2013, Accessed June 24, 2017, https://bangordailynews.com/2013/07/03/news/hancock/acadia-officials-dedicate-renovated-rockefeller-building-at-schoodic-point/

Trotter, Bill, *L.L. Bean Gives Another $1 Million to MDI Bus System*, Bangor Daily News, June 30, 2016, accessed July 3, 2016, https://bangordailynews. com/2016/06/30/news/hancock/l-l-bean-gives-another-1-million-to-mdi-bus-system/

Trotter, Bill, *Rockefeller's will leaves art, millions of dollars, a Maine island*, Bangor Daily News, April 28, 2017, Accessed June 24, 2017, http://goingcoastal. bangordailynews.com/2017/04/28/island-life/david-rockefellers-will-leaves-art-millions-of-dollars-and-an-island-in-maine/

United States, National Park Service. "Acadia National Park (U.S. National Park service)." National Park Service. Accessed March 11, 2017, June 5, 2017, June, 6, 2017, June 7, 2017, June 8, 2017, June 11, 2017, June 22, 2017, June 25, 2017, July 8, 2017, https://www.nps.gov/acad/index.htm

Urban, Sarah 1ˢᵗ class, *End of an Era: NSGA Winter Harbor to Close Its Doors*, Naval Security Group Acitvity Winter Harbor Public Affairs, March, 21, 2002, Accessed June 3, 2017, http://www.navy.mil/submit/display.asp?story_id=1063

Weaver, Jacqueline, Retired Cryptologist Traces Former Naval Base's History, The Ellsworth American, August 1, 2015, accessed January 1, 2017, https://www. ellsworthamerican.com/living/arts-a-living/retired-cryptologist-traces-former-naval-bases-history/

Whynott, Douglas, *Sunrise on Cadillac Mountain*, New England Travel Today, December 28, 2016, Accessed March 11, 2017, https://newengland.com/tag/ sunrise-on-cadillac-mountain/

Non-Publication Sources

Abbe Museum, Bar Harbor, ME, May, 2016

Abbe Museum, Sieur de Monts Nature Center, Acadia National Park, Mt. Desert, ME, May, 2016

Bar Harbor Club, June 2016 & August 2017

Bar Harbor Historical Society, Bar Harbor, June, 2016

Bar Harbor Inn, Bar Harbor, ME, July 2016 & August 2017

Clark, Bill, Lecture, Narrator on Sea Princess Cruise, Northeast Harbor, ME, 2016

Dominy, Lynne, Lecture, Park Ranger, Chief of Interpretation, Acadia National Park, Bar Harbor, ME, 2016

Dorr Museum of Natural History, College of the Atlantic, Bar Harbor, ME, August 2016

Hulls Cove Visitor Center, Acadia National Park, Bar Harbor, ME, June & August 2016

BIBLIOGRAPHY

Islesford Historical Museum, Acadia National Park, Isleford, ME, August, 2016

Kampann, Arthur, Email Correspondence, February, 2016

Kish, Carey, Lecture, Author & Editor, Mt. Desert, ME, 2016

Nature and Sightseeing Cruise, Bar Harbor Whale Watch Co., Bar Harbor, ME, 2016

Robinson, Don, Lecture & Email Correspondence, Mt. Desert, ME, May & June, 2016

Sieur de Monts Nature Center, Acadia National Park, Mt. Desert, ME, May, 2016

Village Green Information Center, Bar Harbor, ME, June, 2016

ABOUT THE AUTHOR

Jeff Alt is an award-winning author, a talented speaker, and a family hiking and camping expert. Alt has been hiking since his youth. In addition to writing the award-winning *Adventures of Bubba Jones* book series, Alt is the author of *Four Boots-One Journey, Get Your Kids Hiking,* and *A Walk for Sunshine. A Walk for Sunshine* won the Gold in the 2009 Book of the Year awards sponsored by Fore Word Reviews; it took first place winner in the 2009 National Best Books Awards Sponsored by USA Book News, and won a Bronze in the 2010 Living Now Book Awards sponsored by Jenkins Group. *Get Your Kids Hiking* won the Bronze in both the 2014 Living Now Book Awards and the 2013 IndieFab Award; in Family and Relationships. Alt is a member of the Outdoor Writers Association of America (OWAA). He has walked the Appalachian Trail, the John Muir Trail with his wife, and he carried his 21-month old daughter across a path of Ireland. Alt's son was on the Appalachian Trail at six weeks of age. Alt lives with his wife and two kids in Cincinnati, Ohio.

For more information about the Adventures of Bubba Jones visit: www.bubbajones.com. For more information about Jeff Alt visit: www.jeffalt.com

E-mail the author: jeff@jeffalt.com

MORE FROM THE BUBBA JONES SERIES

Great Smoky Mountains (2015)

Shenandoah National Park (2016)